The Great Taste
of Straight People

The Great Taste of Straight People

by Lily James

Black Ice
Books

Published by FC2 with support given by the English Department
Unit for Contemporary Literature of Illinois State University,
and the Illinois Arts Council.

Address all inquiries to: FC2, Unit for Contemporary Literature,
Campus Box 4241, Illinois State University, Normal, IL 61790-
4241

The Great Taste of Straight People
Lily James

ISBN: Paper, 1-57366-034-5

Book Design: David A. Dean
Cover Design: Todd Michael Bushman

Produced and printed in the United States of America

for Dobber

Table of Contents

Killer

You probably know a lot about killers, having slept with one. Assuming he left you with more than a location and a time of death. What are the requirements for a good boyfriend anyway? Smart. Funny. Handsome. Not a killer. Never killed anyone. Did not put anyone to death. Had no part in any killings. Didn't kill. Wouldn't kill. Hopes to go his whole life without killing one single person. Heard about killings, but doesn't really know the specifics. Never saw anyone getting killed. Wants to save you from killers. Wants the killers to stay away from you. Thinks killing is wrong. By this reckoning, your last lover was not good boyfriend potential.

He handed you at last a slip of paper. It said:

$$-\frac{2\cancel{c}}{\cancel{a}} = \left(\frac{3x+xa}{b}\right)^{c} - \left(\frac{3x}{b}\right)^{c} - \frac{2\cancel{c}}{\cancel{a}}$$

$$\left(\frac{3x}{b}\right)^{\cancel{c}} = \left(\frac{3x+xa}{b}\right)^{\cancel{c}}$$

$$\frac{3x}{\cancel{b}} = \frac{3x+\cancel{x}a}{\cancel{b}}$$

$$3\cancel{x} = 3\cancel{x} + \cancel{x}a$$

$$\cancel{3} = \cancel{3} + a$$

$$C = a$$

You think that his bad handwriting may suggest an unhealthy mind. Perhaps he was under stress. Perhaps he was holding a gun on you. Perhaps you were holding a gun on him. Perhaps there was no gun at all more a threat of a gun. You realize that this will not be what one would normally call a real date, more an invitation to the place where he's doing the killing. You're going to do the standing around looking shocked part, or perhaps the bleeding hemorrhaging dying part. You'll do the part people usually do even if they are not informed ahead of time in the form of a math problem. But because of your warning you aspire to another role, a role of savior. You will be duplicitous. That is what you immediately think. You want to save the dead person from being dead. You believe A to be someone you know who is important, or perhaps, or definitely, actually, it is you. C is someone else powerful, B may be some divisive traitor in your basement, D and E a couple where E likes to be on top. Therefore E is female or male. Or E is two people and D is very very happy.

You switch apartments, move to a duplex which may place you in base 2, and sell your car. In this way you can perhaps stop being A and take on a new variable, M or N, those being popular, or you could become a Greek letter, a real function. But still, even if he could not immediately find you, that piece of paper would still be in his hand and in your hand, and he would still see the A and that equals 0 and you would still be dead. Attempted murderers serve what ten years? But successful murderers get more? Less? Should he really be rewarded for fucking up possibly the most important action of his life? You decide to leave a message: Hey, if he got me, he got me. You feel like maybe that is being too generous but comfort yourself that it will not be admissible in court. It will just be for him to know that you really understood and that you were there for him in the end. For money, you have begun taking in laundry, having quit your job in order to disappear. Doing laundry as a profession is still possible and real, even after its great romanticization in old novels. You obsess on the constancy of some things. You realize at your highest level of concentration that moving or changing your name isn't going to change the numerical value of A or anything else ephemeral. The minute he wrote that equation he was in your house with a gun, saying Down your neck.

You are brooding on who is who. Perhaps C= your friend Chris because obviously the name begins with C and then he was owed some money and achieved a certain status or power. B=the old downstairs neighbor. Perhaps D and E are Cece and Rick. They're certainly negative. You call up Cece, tell her to be careful but don't say why. Hope she prods, but she doesn't have time. Says she'll call you later. You remind her she doesn't have your new number. She says then why don't you call HER back. You think of going back to an old boyfriend, but he would think you were a cheater. You realize that math is math. If A=0 then that's all. Time passes.

The math problem accompanies you to lunch, takes out your trash, straightens your pillowcases before you sleep. You work the equation until every possible combination of multiply by this divide and by that has proven to you that you are always 0. Variables drop out on both sides. Numbers fall away. You can make it as complicated as you like going upwards, adding variables and friends, but when you go down, solving for A, there you are dead. Helpless. You can't even divide by yourself. You can't add yourself. Nothing changes, and you think he has forgotten all about you. He calls you.

HI! you say gladly. It would do no good to be given a death threat and then not killed. Picking you out for slaughter and then just sort of forgetting about you is probably a very bad insult, from a murderer. If you were TRULY important or pressing, he would have killed you as soon as possible. Hello he says. I'm doing okay, you say. Kind of scared but not really.

While he is on his way over you nervously call up your friends and suggest that they change their essential natures. For example, they could vary once in a while. On this side of the equals sign they could be positive, and on the other side negative. Just a change, a little skip in the monotonous march of absolute value. Your friends are rigid. They laugh indulgently at themselves and how they see everything so black and white. They make excuses as if it were an issue of cholesterol level. You point out in a cleverly subtle way that if an equation were to be written in which you were all aligned in a very particular way then they would all cancel each other out, and drop out entirely, leaving you there feeling like a modestly proud survivor but also rather vulnerable. You think you hear them saying something about how if you would just get your real value finally mercilessly exposed then they could all be happy because even if it means they have to drop like flies that's FINE they say because AT LEAST YOU'LL BE GONE. You know that can't be right. You ask What? but he is knocking at the door. He kills you with a rope. Taking three minutes to strangle you dead. Him being in the equation Mr. X of course, married to melodrama.

The Sister and the Stoop

Once we had the idea to set our sister out on the stoop, and prevent her from returning to the house. We thought this would help with the problem of her meanness, and her apparent desire to turn each of the family into a lying two-faced bitch. Cindy did the job quickly, she carried our sister by force out onto the lonely stoop, there dropped her flat. While she was recuperating from the fall Cindy slammed the door that became the lockout for our sister henceforth. Our sister was not happy or pleased in the least about her new quarters. She seemed to believe her cries of rage and terrible threats could make us take her in, but it only convinced us that we had made the right decision in putting her out there, and we told her through the mail slot that some nice man would be around directly to marry her and take her away, and we tried to sound encouraging, even though we felt only rage. And she said what about dinner, and we looked at each other with distasteful smiles. Our sister loved food. To excess.

I BLAME CINDY THE MOST BUT YOU ARE ALL WHORES cried our sister through the mail slot. We had been trying to sleep for hours. We could not even imagine what people must think, except that they had unruly sisters of their own and were jealous of our cleverness. Our sister was a trollish type, and could sleep anywhere. We found her refusal to sleep to be insubordinate and rude. Finally Cindy dropped a skunk bomb out onto the stoop and the stunning blast convinced our sister to curl up as if dead. Viewing her from the upstairs window as we were, her ass was shoved into the air violently as her face was knocked against the stoop and stuck there, and she snored. It was a mercy not to have that snoring right up against our faces in the night. We slept like queens.

The next morning our sister was so hungry that she talked of foraging throughout the neighborhood for little boys who weren't so quick on their feet. She said she would develop a taste for the small ones who were dull or retarded, and would come to consider it a mission. She would have to talk to their parents later and most would not seem grateful. Getting away with murder was the least of it, we felt. The cold water bags in the bottom of the refrigerator had taken up too much space, and the cornnuts stashed in the bottom of our beds had made our feet itch and burn. A terrible sister is a burden beyond the scope of most burdens. It is a terrible burden.

Morning was when she usually made the food that would last all day and in her absence dear Betty had to cook steak sandwiches and coffee. By ten o'clock she had given up. Poor Betty was the weakest in spirit, but the beauty of her astounded most visitors, and her marriage proposals filled a small box in the hall. Cindy had friends and a talent for gardening, Maria felt sorry for herself and wrote long letters to members of the social scene, and Darice collected money. We were all grand and glorious women. Betty, Cindy, Maria, Darice, and Horror. It is not difficult to decipher which of us was bound to be a failure. Our terrible sister had raised such a clamor for food that we could not read our books in the morning after breakfast. RAISIN CAKE APPLE PIE DELICIOUS STRAWBERRIES AND MILK AND DOUGH-NUTS she wailed piteously. Her knees were tucked under the stoop and her elbows were pressed on it as if praying. The matted hair around her ears had not been washed and we knew if she were with us the smell of it would make us gag more than usual. She was NOXIOUS and we HATED HER! Cindy shoved doughnuts through the mail slot and our sister in her hurry put her mouth up to it so that Cindy had to shove hard to get it all down her. Our wonderful house was stained with the dark blood of doughnuts. It was a two-story house and painted white with blue shutters. Maria worked very hard to keep the house clean, expecting nothing in return. Darice was generous with gifts from her piles of money in the basement. That stupid sister didn't even keep any doughnuts for later on. She was not one to think ahead in this way. She preferred gluttony and starvation.

YOU HAVE TO COME OUT SOMETIME AND THEN YOU WILL FACE ME AND I WILL EAT YOUR EYES OUT OF YOUR HEAD AND I WILL SHIT ON YOUR STOMACHS AND WALK AWAY AND THE SHIT JUICE WILL RUN DOWN INTO YOUR PUSSIES AND YOU WILL BE CON-TAMINATED NO MAN IN HIS RIGHT MIND WOULD WANT TO FUCK YOU AND YOU WILL ALSO HAVE HAD YOUR HANDS RIPPED OFF FROM YOUR BODY AND THROWN ONTO TRUCKS AND THEY WILL BE TAKEN FAR AWAY NO HOPE OF REATTACHMENT AND YOU WILL HAVE YOUR BLIND HANDLESS SHIT PUSSIES IN JAIL BEFORE I AM DONE she screamed.

All of us wondered individually about how she could prolong this screaming without any water. Then we remembered the side spigot. Darice knew the basement well and knew which hoses and nozzles to cut and which just went off into the ground. We followed her down with torches to discover a way by which we could choke our sister effectively. We were not surprised at our distrust of each other. At any moment some one of us could crack and open the door and all would be lost. The decision to put your sister on the stoop is not one which can be revoked. She will not say coming in OH I KNOW IT WAS ONLY IN FUN once the water has been turned off and the doughnuts have stopped their squishing through the brass mail slot. She will not forgive. Darice clamped her tool down onto a large brown hose and when she had squeezed it shut she wound a rope around it to hold it. We were all carrying knives to prevent insurrection. Darice's knife was in a clever satchel hung off of her leather belt. The desperation in such a move was evident.

It was not long before we heard the wail of torment burst from our sister's lips as she twisted the spigot in terror. YOU FOUL SLUTS she sighed loudly. THE WATER'S GONE OFF AND YOU DON'T EVEN KNOW IT. We giggled for a while and then snuggled down in the den to take naps in the afternoon. When we awoke, we heard the scratching. All knew the truth. The door was under attack with her claws and that bitch was scratching at the door wanting in or to break or to break her hands. Maria began to cry and we pulled our knives on her in silent agreement. DO YOU WANT TO BE NEXT said Cindy in a hostile knife-carrying way. Maria snivelled and we knew she was weak in the head

Lily James

and could be expected to crack at any moment. Yet she knew too many people. People we needed to see socially. The Martin Smythe-Farthingtons. The James Monnington-Browns. And so on. Soon she felt sorry for her display and came around with a plan. Going to the door she opened it out and closed it fiercely several times until our bad sister had been bludgeoned by the door enough to sit down hard on her butt in failure. We hugged Maria and laughingly forgave.

Yet there was a problem. We hadn't gotten food enough to last her out. Somehow we had planned that she would wander off or be stolen, but now we had to breach her guard on the house and get off to the grocery. Cindy knew how. Our last box of doughnuts was placed in a crate which she lowered from the roof down into that horrible woman's range of sight. When she had grabbed at it firmly, strong Cindy lifted her high off the ground so she would be afraid to let go anyway eating the doughnuts with one hand she had to hang on. Darice scurried out into the yard and bolted down the street carrying her pretty purse and no one saw. It was a triumph! Once in town she could buy a helicopter and that would settle the problem. The roof had a large flat space on it right behind the attic. We loved our house for its helpful ways.

Soon people passed in parades to see the sister that had been vanquished so severely from the house. Most shook their heads and muttered but we knew they would not take her home so why? Others got excited about it and threw bits of concrete and metal at our sister who had come to be known as a mountain man by some, as a hermaphrodite by others. We could not control her public image from the house, and since Darice was the only one who could fly the helicopter, she was the only one who talked to the press. She was shy. She made up something about the plague. It was a bad idea.

After several days while we saw our sister drinking out of a puddle and shitting off the curb we became too bold and taunted her from the house. SEE NOW HOW DUMB YOU ARE STUPID HORROR we yelled and threw her doughnuts but into a pile of dirt or water. She scurried her nasty legs all hairy now and pitted with mosquito bites. YOU THOUGHT YOU COULD OUTLIVE US DIDN'T YOU we said. She snarled and slapped at the bugs that annoyed her and scratched her face with her claws leaving unsightly gashes under the eyes. When we couldn't think of any more things to taunt her with we started telling her to go out into the world with her ugly face and her disastrous perm. DON'T FORGET TO WRITE said Cindy in a mean sarcastic tone. Our sister had no soul and never cried in fact she laughed and stomped around the sidewalk chanting about how she would get back in there and we would love her. She even tried to brush out her hair and smile at us. We almost gagged.

That night, Betty had a pang of conscience. She and Maria had been talking about how we couldn't have any parties now and they seemed in agreement that this sister incident must be brought to a close. They were both young and still liked men. The older sisters liked to drink at parties and did not deny that the fun had gone out of the house. Betty used the telephone to call up John who was the nicest man we knew. We also knew that John was expecting a transfer to Idaho. Our sister has fallen on hard times we said.

Wouldn't you like to come and see her. We agreed that after this step had been taken, we would have done all we could and that the next step was to stone her to death on the lawn. CLEAN YOURSELF UP we shouted through the mail slot at our snoring sister. THERE IS A MAN COMING TO SEE YOU TONIGHT. Maria went so far as to toss a see-through dress out the upstairs window. But there are stones in the basement Darice assured us. Somehow we thought that we could kill her silently and without much trouble. Why she had not wandered off by now was a terrible mystery. We could not believe it.

John arrived and told his driver to drive around the block a few times so as not to intimidate our sister who was now believed to have been raised by wolves. She wore the dress even though it had popped out at one side seam. The grass matted into her hair made it seem thicker and she had smeared her hands with wormies to make them soft. Good evening said our coy and useless sister to the man. You are so kind to come and call. We were all smashed up against the kitchen window hoping to see a few things. She began by toying with his lapel and clearly had redemption in mind when she kissed his shoe and rubbed off the kiss with her sleeve. John was charmed. You have to give her credit said Betty and then we kicked her until she was silent. Our sister looked so bad and stupid in her dress and her ugly body that she almost looked good. The word cute could not have been applied but perhaps the word sublime.

John said that he liked the way she stroked him on the pants and she said that she had been reading about certain pagan cults and they got into an interesting conversation sitting on the lawn. We snickered when she pointed her chin down to make her face look thinner and we poked each other when he put a hand on her shoulder and squeezed its ugliness. The grass in her hair sparkled in the sun and the dead donut flecks nestled in her teeth distractingly. She giggled and nodded when he said so I am a business man and she said I am intrigued by the works of people world-wide. They were getting along well, and the people walking by smiled fondly and gave them the thumbs up.

When John had our sister in his car he waved his thanks to us in the window and we waved back hopefully. She might have died out there. She might have come to a bad end. Driving away we clearly made out the snarling face of our sister speaking words of hate through the back window at us. It made us smile. She was, after all, gone. We sat down in our comfortable den and made plans for a new party and how we might repair the yard.

Jane Breaks the Cot

When summer comes Ellen wants to go on a trip with a woman and she tells Janie she wants to go with her.

Let's go up north she says *My Dad had this cottage up there when I was growing up in the Upper Peninsula and we went in the summers, it's right on the lake but you have to go down the road to the dock if you want to go swimming because the part right in front of the cottage has reeds in it and is shallow.*

Janie says yes and it's okay with her husband to go with Ellen that mean old friend. He gives her a big chocolate cake for the road and kisses her on the forehead goodbye. Then they are leaving and it is really goodbye to everyone.

Bye, he says, *eat up the whole thing. Call me from Kalamazoo. Call me from Traverse City. Call me from the gas station on the way into town. It's made with vanilla pudding but it's chocolate. Here's a knife to cut it up, and you can share a piece with Ellen. Here's a plate. Don't swim too much. Don't drown.*

Ellen and Jane get in the car and drive and Ellen takes some marijuana along and Jane thinks well I certainly won't be smoking any of that.

Couple of girls like you, says the gas station guy in Detour, Michigan, *you're not from around here are you? You're from Ohio aren't you? You're from the university at Sault Saint Marie. You want a nice vacation? Rent yourself a cottage from Marcel Prete on Caribou Lake.*

Ellen pays for the gas like she's been doing even though Alan gave Jane ten dollars. Jane can't finish the cake and it's getting mushy.

We used to call that pisswater lake because it's warm, that silly old fuck, it's late, it's dark, we'll just stop by Dan Opulka's house. Dad told me the last time he went fishing he took Dan and he asked about me [Ellen smiles] *I used to date him when I was in high school. I used to date a lot of people up here.*

Jane thinks yeah I could tell you some stories self righteous tea sipping bitch. She has not talked to Ellen in this fashion. Ellen is more proud in the house in Ann Arbor. Ellen has liked people. Jane is glad to be out of that house. Stopping at Dan Opulka's house must be something that dumb Ellen wants to do.

When I was in high school I fucked around a lot too, says Jane *It was fun and I started keeping a list of who I still had to get fucked by. One time my teacher found the list and told some of the boys that I had crushes on them. I could do handsprings all the way from the front door to the gymnasium. I could do a backflip off the auditorium stage.*

Jane settles herself in the seat and throws the rest of the cake out the window. The road is so narrow and made out of hard sand and tiny rocks in the headlights she can see the trees and bushes hanging into the road, and the two ruts for the car to go in. What happens if somebody comes to pass? Ellen smiles at her as if she forgives her. Ellen looks small in the big brown car and they both are small, they're short girls.

When we get to Dan's house, says Ellen, *you'll stay in the car while I go in.*

Quiet car, they're in the country, it's different and she can tell the lake is near because of the type of vegetation there is there, and the sand. She can smell the lake and the smell is making her happy.

Here, says Ellen and they pull into a yard, bunches of cars in a row, dogs tied to the trees. It's misty kind of, a chill, it's almost raining now, *I think this is the house, maybe, I think this is where it is.*

Ellen goes in to maybe Dan's house. Janie is still smelling and looking around as if she's never been anywhere but that crummy house and now here she is out of it. It smells fresh, but that could be the rain. She wants to get out of the car.

In the red neck bar with Dan Opulca. He's nice but maybe dumb and reminds Janie of high school and because of that arouses her. There's hardly anyone in there, movie set, gold vinyl seat literally gold textured vinyl, and red table tops. They drink beer and liquor and buy each other rounds. Ellen is amazing, can't say anything, she's making her eyes soft and playing with her glass, she must be flirting. Jane takes over.

How many things do you kill in for example a week she says to Dan who is aware enough to laugh but still answers her and then laughs again to show he is onto her. He likes her. Dan is soft looking and works in construction with his buddy. He's really white and tall and if he's young she's younger, but she might have wrinkles starting and he doesn't. He's been fed right all along.

A tourist fisherman asks Dan to play pool and he says yes and the girls drape themselves over the booths, alluring, witty, making jokes with the rednecks and the fishermen. Mostly Ellen is trying to be at Dan's elbow and drunk. Janie finds this really funny, and goes about stealing him, back in the old style, back in it all the way. She controls the jukebox. She controls the northwest corner of the pool table with her crotch rubbing against it. There in the redneck bar with Patsy Cline on the jukebox she gets Dan to look over. A football player, soccer, anyone. She drinks out of Dan's bottle casually and hold his cue while he goes to the men's room. Ellen puts her hair in front of her shoulders and looks more feminine, but isn't quite drunk enough Janie thinks. Good.

Let's go driving, she says, *Ellen can drive.*

Because Janie lies that she has never been skinny dipping they do that, off the dock which is down the road from Ellen's parents' cabin. They can see lights on the shore and the inside lights of the car they drove all the way out on the dock, not supposed to, left the door open. Janie strips down fast and slides into the water, letting the rough wood touch her and she watches Ellen thinking that Ellen was a beautiful young girl here in this town that no one could have. Ellen has a tank top for a bra and she leaves that on until she gets in the water, she's hanging off the dock with one hand, with her feet on the ladder and she pulls the top off with the other hand and throws it up there and makes a splash in the lake.

Janie's floating way out pretending not to be there. She can see the boy Dan Opulka with his nice but unused body and thin underwear. She is reminded there was this time she was running through the woods on their farm in Pennsylvania and the neighbors had three teenaged boys. They had to go down in the well and fix something that was messed up down in there, and took turns in their trunks going down on a rope while the other ones stood there shivering their whole bodies shaking and wet. She always feels protective of men who are cold. Dan gets into the water boldly as if he has never had a problem with being naked. Jane feels his body in the water and feels that he wants her not Ellen who is doing a sedate kind of sidestroke by the dock.

Jane lets her breasts rise above the water and can still hear them saying they're cold, it's cold water, she's too drunk to know if she is or not, she can hear the shore a long way back and see lights, but she loves it when the moon makes shadows and it is full, lighting up Dan's dark head and Ellen's long floating hair getting closer. Dan looks at Janie and she feels her breast circles above the water's surface and lets her hips break the water too.

They have to get in the cottage and the electric is turned off.

Come with me, says Ellen.

Here's the hallway and the toilet and sink, this must be the main room, *Dad's left things in the way and no flashlights I can find,* the girls hold hands and Janie wants Ellen to tell her every step, *the door to the garage is over at the other side of the room, that's the sofa, if I could just get this wood off the windows, here stand here and hold onto this and don't move I'm going to try and get the wood off this window,* Jane imagines the room as cavernous like garages are with naked floors and walls stripped bare, echoing, a big kitchen fireplace that sucks the heat out of the house, she is at one corner of an enormous room that you can't crawl across in a day, Ellen grunts and strains at the whatever and bangs on it, *shit,* they'll have to crawl back through the garage, no light, knee high, big cold sheets of glass, the eyes open or the eyes shut it doesn't matter.

Dan drops sweat in a stream off his elbow directly onto Janie's nipples. He's on the higher level of sauna and she's below him on her back laughing. They have a dipper and a bucket of water to pour on the rocks in the middle stove and mostly Ellen does that, putting her other hand out to balance herself over the stove. They've been smoking the pot, all of them have. *What are you going to tell the boys about Ellen,* asks Jane. *I don't know,* he says, he's cute giggling and shy, and he passes them the bottle of liquor which they're now drinking absolutely straight. It would be a disaster to get sober now, after they've got themselves here to the sauna. Ellen plays it off and asks about different ones and Dan gives the answers and keeps making Janie laugh in different ways. He doesn't want to actually touch her but he makes the sweat do it, and acts brave. *I'm ruined,* Ellen jokes to them, *don't tell my father I was naked with you Dan.* Janie puts her hand up and it's a delicate nice hand and she splashes the drop when it's in the air, back up to get him instead. *Jane he's dripping sweat on your nipples,* says Ellen, *don't you care?*

For the girls there's the sofa bed to pull out and put the comforter on and for him there's a cot from the garage. Janie kicks the cot. He's now just laughing and looking at her because he doesn't have to do anything when she's doing it, and Ellen says *come on let's go to bed*, and Janie kicks at the cot so it falls over. Ellen stands it back up and tosses him a blanket playfully and tells him to can it and go to bed, Ellen goes in the kitchen being careful to brush her teeth.

Janie gets out of bed deliberately and eyes him standing there clutching the blanket. The room is full of antiques, small and close, brick smooth floor and little tiny fireplace that doesn't work, toaster oven, shelves for food, a sewing machine that looks rusty. Dan Opulka shifts his feet and grins at her and Janie smashes the cot with her naked foot until there's no way to make it stand up.

Ellen comes in and Janie's in bed with Dan. *Looks like he'll have to sleep between us* says Jane. Dan might already be asleep. Who will he turn his face to - who wins the night?

In the middle of the night he works up the balls to touch her and rubs her arm up and down softly with one finger but she's not asleep and notices and pushes against him happily and he does it. They take him home the next day in the car, not saying much but that they won't forget this soon in Detour will they?

Janie and Ellen sit on the white sunny roof of the grandmother's boat house in the reedy messy part of the lake in front of the cabin where you can't swim. They're talking about writing a movie they might write it about two lovers and one of them the man is married and when the other one is rowing past his house she sees him with his wife beating her up and she's pregnant and the girl just keeps on rowing and leaves even though she really loved him. Or it could be about a girl who helped this boy fix his boat and fell in love. That could be a good scene there for the beginning. They figure out the soundtrack who they would have on it. They spot a ship coming and are quite absorbed in watching it come when they are suddenly on their butts in a ∟oot of water they have broken grandmother's boat house and they're wet. It seems like they are still sitting up there and just thought they fell in, but they have to get themselves out, sloppy boots and mud, reeds in their clothes. Were they too fat to sit up there? Ellen's the skinniest girl. Janie sits still in the terrible water and her chest shakes and she starts crying and for no reason she can't stop crying. Ellen pulls her hair back from her face and looks at the tears. She puts her arms around Janie and says *don't be sad it's just an old boat house. Grandma won't be angry, she'll just get Dad to fix it.* Janie cries more and more and Ellen rocks her back and forth and puts her head down on Janie's bent over hair and she sighs and says *It's just an old boat house.*

Ellen and Jane drive back to the house in Ann Arbor. When Janie gets out and takes her bag out of the trunk, Ellen carries it in. They tell other people to go get the rest of the stuff out of the car. They order other people around for days.

Split

To her there is marriage. This favorite need of a woman who does not stray. She's on the bed in the sex fat house fingering the diaphragm. She's put in several starchy sponges like rolaids and spermicide, in the past. Toward positioning and elimination. She gets a kick out of it. The thing about marriage is, the two become one. And those two, that become one, are to be joined as two. To become. Putting her fingers under the covers and over the covers.

if she were to die it would be by fire. if she were to extinguish it would be by glamor and flame. standing on the roof it would erupt between her legs, and with one hand on the roof vent of the heaters, one arm flung toward heaven, she would be shot upward slightly as the licking came through the roof exploding up from under. it would be a chemical fire. she would be able to see the rift approaching across the roof. and would have just enough time to assume she would die burning. the night sky over her deadens it directly. she sinks only singed into the fire legs still splayed and arms clutching bits of tar paper flaming.

"you were most likely a witch in one of your former

lives" says the diviner.

In this way she learned the inherent tragic symmetry of the human body, which would appear to her escapable by nothing but death. But to lay him out for sex when he arrived was easy and was uncomplicated.

Here is Pennsylvania and a camp meeting grounds six miles west of Puncsatawny. Her father stands full of cancer in the second quadrant (- , +) at the podium of the taber-nacle. Grounds bisected by the ravine which is parallel to route 80, and the main road which goes from tents through dormitories to permanent cabins, passing by the young people's tabernacle and the large public outhouse, rising over the ravine in a bridge where the young people congre-gate at dusk, after their prayer meeting. Here is Illinois with Chicago in the Northeast corner, bisected by 94 and 290. Alan stands full of colitis in the fourth quadrant (+ , -) at the podium in a basement at the University of Chicago sur-rounded by rapt socialists whose elbows stick out onto metal and formica tables that make a square. Each socialist on the same side of the table as Alan has to twist his head 90 degrees to see him and hear him correctly. Each socialist on the connecting sides must twist his head an average of 45 degrees to see him correctly. Of course the socialist directly across from Alan does not have to twist, but can look straight ahead, making a line with his eyes which cuts the table in two around them.

She is aware that there are two ways to combine these

two maps. In one combination the belly button represents
Toledo, and Puncsatawny lies to the east, Chicago to the
west and north. So the torso would perform the task of
representing some part of America, which makes a certain
kind of sense, in a general and diseased way. However, she
determines that the more ingenuous plan is to lay the two
maps over each other, so that the belly button represents
(approximately) both the Sears Tower and the bridge over
the ravine, positioning the father and Alan in roughly
opposite locations, but giving a more accurate picture
overall. Now the Chicago basement, lying over the large
intestine, and the Pennsylvania tabernacle, left lung, can be
clearly delineated. In the Chicago basement, the question
of whether the myth of democracy only exists to satiate the
human desire for autonomy created by the lure of a capitalist economy, in the tabernacle a call to the mission field and
a promise of crowns in paradise. Stop paying lip service to
the devil. It is possible to live an absolute life. His skin crawls
in anticipation.

Tracing this plan onto herself, she finds that the source
of the egg must be the left ovary. If both ovaries produce
then there is competition and confusion. If the right ovary
produces (quadrant three) there is disease. If the right ovary
produces an egg, there is faith and no wife beating. Horrible
to think of the randomness under which she could be
operating. Compromise. She contracts the muscles in her
left buttock very quickly, encouraging the advent of an egg.
If she feels it coming out the wrong side she will shut it
down. She has counted days and degrees. She can do that again.

With his body spread out in this way on the bed she allows her breasts to make what shapes they will on both sides of his sternum two circles. Awe can be inspired in Puncsatawny and Chicago. To bite the rib cage fervently or to slowly drive the tongue in circles down the groin she spans really the entire southeast side almost to Indiana, while arousing points along the ravine and on up past the Franklin cabin into the woods. She spreads her fingers behind his shoulder blades and licks the hollow behind the collar bone, one breast hovering over the tabernacle, one hip bone planted firmly in Hyde Park. Alan is on pain killers, his ulcer is in action, his ulcer is to be avoided. She moves up so when the penis comes up it presses into her thigh between leg and leg it pushes itself into that space. Suddenly there is a chalk artist and a puppet show at the young people's tabernacle, and the discussion level at Alan's conference has risen to the level of the illuminati, it would seem, how best to reprogram the world, how best indeed.

The first thing to be done by her is to shut off the colitis and ulcer. To create a cavity where the arthritis and the digestive disorders can coagulate peacefully somewhere in the third quadrant (- , -). This involves a realignment of the stomach to the other side of the x axis, counting the body as planar algebra, and not Euclid. Looking down at the torso it is a simple shift, then some sort of membrane which is permeable to of course gas, but not to any kind of virus or sperm. Of course the sperm/anti-sperm ratio being disturbed by this isolation, some osmotic interaction could result. She terms it negligible. The sperm are down in the testicles anyway.

The difference between the two maps on their stomachs pressed together is that one is not a mirror image. They do not coincide. To her it seems easier to turn around and fuck him backwards, looking down at his feet and with her ass to his face because this would make clear the left right distinction and she would not be able to mess it up. But in her moment of power she is not tempted to degrade him. When she has worked out all this to achieve some say and to call in some higher power, to call up a third party, she is not willing to allow any victory to make her sour. She is used to fucking on top, and there is no reason to fuck ass backwards.

There comes the tearing when the dick goes in her, familiar, desire to be struck. Here is the image of him pounding up through her and the wickedness exposed, burned, and sunk. Dividing the left ovary from the right he can separate out that witch that won't think for herself from the good happy woman making wise decisions and he can send himself into the diaphragm anyway, unwilling to commit semen to one with the other there jeering. He is on top again pushing away at her, attempting to reach her throat, uncareful which hipbone gets the most weight, so she pulls him into a kiss and rights herself to slow him down before he ruins everything.

Look, she says about his mind, he can amaze and defend and offend. She likes to think of him talking to the socialists who can follow where he has been but he jumps ahead while the smartest ones walk sturdily behind. What has been said about the father is that his sermons are so densely cross referenced, who can conceive of the Bible in this complicated way, everyone says. He keeps them on the edge of their seats, it is said. And sick. And without notes. Here is Alan been throwing up blood, here is father so grey and losing one pound for every day. Holding them. Here is the new x axis connecting Puncsatawny to Chicago, and here is the new y axis connecting genitals to brain, and the dick is a vector in the plane of z, with end coordinates: (0,-5,0), (0,-5,5). Her planes and vectors are of course less stable, but when it comes to a question of priority, the genital to brain channel must be clean, straight, and clever. No buildup. No letdown.

There is a terrible sadness in her. As she lowers her hips down onto him she is conscious of the shift left, the movement of right to left to turn the vector into the fourth quadrant (puncsatawny, chicago, pancreas) and out of the third quadrant (colitis, cancer, nobleness and error). After the angle is achieved, she is sweating and he pants, there is only to draw the vector repeatedly into the z plane and out, the collision of systems bending to destroy and create the vector as far as it gets it becomes monumental, arrow to the left ovary which bulbs and produces bulb. At the moment when the agitation is so great in the womb and fatherstuff, there is great revival and great hope in the meeting hall, great determination in the basement. She can make it seem like this the socialists coming to the altar and the funda- mentalists waving union signs, and drawing a strong black line down the x axis from the brain, she pulls it up through the vector, leaving it flat and wrinkled on the horizontal plane, and pulling it on up into her body. And Janie, sick with cancer and absolutely ill with colitis, having recently taken hard and dangerous drugs, conceives a child.

if she were to be killed on the water, the river raft would be split in two the rapids, mountains chasms rising up on either side, only sunlight sharp and undiluted by air coming down on her small raft she had been clutching with her arms, to hit and skid over a protruding rock, causing a split in the shiny skin, leaving her left leg on a different piece from her right. then the legs would strain at pulling together the pieces, the legs would ravenously struggle with the water's chaotic pull. one groan echoes up through the layers of rock and desert and is rushed over by the cracking of wood against wood, and her legs are dragged toward each other into the water, or they are so strong that they remain on the raft bits and her body is torn begun there and carried up through to her head.

"most likely you were killed while they tried to figure out if you were a witch" the diviner says.

Vivisection, Vivisection, Where's Your Erection?

Maybe Kate was fainting on purpose. Perhaps she felt it was earned drama for someone who had approached the blue cold eyes of truth, or whatever thing she was calling it, or maybe she was just interested in the way she could fall to the floor while still concious and still have all the "i feel fragile and small" consequences in her body. People who faint. People who die trying. People who are too ill and weak and not of this world to EVEN STAND. Gina was standing, watching her, poolside, when it supposedly happened. Kate had been in the swimming pool with Gina on top and above her up there making splashies and being cutie with everyone else from the office and Kate was down there with her feet scraping the unclean tile and she said later that it merged on her that a clear choice would be to either Rise or Stay Down. She said she opened her eyes and could see the fractured surface above her bubbling with activity. It was so blue and cold and eyes came out of the wall to see her and meet with her. This being told to a cluster of followers and panting men as if it had not been purposefully laid out to be a dramatic moment. As if it just happened that way. And when they dragged her up she tried to make it obvious she had lost all her ways of getting back out of it. Like when you say *OH NEVER MIND* and then the person does really never mind. You're fucked. Like Kate was saying *maybe I will not*

*rise no never just leave them up there to bubble and me down here
to stare into this and pry at my suit.* Then they had to drag her.

The next time this bullshit occurred Gina and Kate were
in a gallery together. It was there in a gallery, and the people
around them might have been unaware or perhaps blown
apart by the winds, but as it came Kate knew Where and
Here she would be sucked back down if not linked purposefully to some hearty soul who was very unconnected to the
whole "real actual honest to god truth" vibe. She chose
Gina, who was apparently now being seen as some fleshy
ugly person usable by Kate to keep her deep oh so immortal
soul from plunging to the depths of perception and painful
clarity. Of course Kate could have run or could have NOT
said *Hey do you want to make out real quick.* Anyway then Kate
was on the floor unbuttoning her clothes but seeming like
she really didn't want to do it but apparently there was an
obvious need. *Oh Gross* said Kate softly gritting her teeth
when Gina's mouth went around her tit and found some
soft secretion actually a globby lump and Gina simulta-
neously thinking *it's your goddamn tit* and *so this is what
females do.* Leaning down into the hip part she was firmly
rooted there in the gutter of the bones and the skin, and
truth passed over looking down its cold blue eyes with the
shudder of thunder. Which was when Kate started passing
out at work, when they said poser and mocked it, but there
she was lying flat, uncomposed, martyred, true. And no one
could say ANYTHING.

Once in the bathtub Gina felt wet. Once in the lake she
felt herself sinking. Maybe it was Kate who kept feeling her
physical nastiness and keeping her out of the mind. It is sad
to use someone to keep you disgusted. It's not polite. Kate

is not polite. *This shall not be a road movie* said Gina. *Do you think I know nothing of cinema just because I sucked your pussy to distract you do you think I am not an artist. I LIVE IN THE UKRAINIAN VILLAGE. SEE ME.*

Gina had always been operating under the principle of "as long as you are thinner than your fattest friend, you're fine." Kate seemed to operate on some other principle, that allowed her to be much much thinner than Gina. It was annoying to try and decipher the different paradigms. It would be easier to slice her open and get at that globby brain. Of course you can't have two friends operating on that principle. One would disappear first. And win. Can't be letting that happen in these days when winning turns into someone else starving at the hands of your dreadful tyranny. You can't be LEFT BEHIND. You can't be sitting there WATCHING a revelation. Someone breathing in heated paroxysms of wealthy heavy truth and you just breathing in smoke? Here's Kate. Now what are you going to do with a girl like this besides vivisection? She just cuts so damn easy, with little flakes of everdry skin lifting off the edge of the knife in satisfying curls. It's not bad to vivisect your friends. And Kate wasn't even a friend, merely using her for a vagina in a time of truth. Someone told her that hair dye has plastic in it to make the hair shiny. Seems like a nice idea, but then it also kills the hair follicle and ruins the head of hair. So, applying this principle to Kate, vivisection seemed obvious.

Gina tells Kate firmly that it is her boyfriend Dogboy whose cigarette breath melds with her cigarette breath in such a way as to negate them both and turn them into fruits. *Once while I was kissing him in a car I drew up alongside Truth, Truth in its responsible wagon sedan. And it was only his tongue and my tongue meeting and wrenching each other and feeling mossy and ugly that kept me from strangling on that truthy wagon and puking up into his mouth and being dead and gone lost in it horrible melted rotted old rag.* Kate is unconvinced, and feels that Gina has never had visions, and will never. That Gina is as she puts it a loss.

She's saying *confusing ideas with message* and Kate can see why she's saying that and then says *theme is sort of the same thing* and then Gina says but *you have to consider intent.* They are having a literary argument at work to make Kate feel bad. Kate has not done the reading. *I'll think it through in great detail and come up with great ideas on an outline that you're going to kill anyway* said Kate and Gina thought Wait, that's my style. She thinks she can take credit for inventing wasted labor. *I'm just too hurt and betrayed and killed to even think or worry about this,* she says back. *I'll have to leave it with you and come back to it on Monday when I've had an entire weekend of not sleeping and moping around pressing up against Dogboy in soft sleep. I'm too ugly and tired to deal with you right now.*

Gina I prefer to wear incredibly irrationally too-big stockings to my job. I think that it really causes my coworkers to question the whole put-together perfect girl image that they have been taught to expect from girls of my age and weight. I think it causes them to personally deconstruct their prescription for fashion success. Me hitching and scratching and hootching and sneaking behind this or that wall to do a complete stocking overhaul. Given forty feet of floor, my stockings can creep and slide all the way down to my ankle. Wait until you see it. You'll be APPALLED. But it's not my fault. It's Kate.

Kate   I don't want to be given a sharp knife and told to strip when I am already naked. I don't think that is a reasonable request. Look, I'm just a person who happened to wear torn-up jeans to work one day. She's the one with the lust for the truth serum. I'm nobody's antibody. But I do have this theory. You see, coffee is always this drink that people have at their desks. Simple. A cup. But the choice should be made for soda or water, not coffee. I have studied and determined that the rate at which coffee gets cold (undrinkable) is much faster than the rate at which soda gets warm or flat (undrinkable). So why people must want coffee at their desks is to continue the already hostile process of stress on the job. Drink it faster, get it done, be ready for your next cup on time. It's a bad choice. This has been a message from the Soda Drink Foundation Society of which I am a paid spokesperson.

Gina   <sigh>

Kate   But the bare essence of it all is that I don't want my skin to be removed. You can reduce the whole system to that. You can take everything in my life and pare it down, shearing off concentric circles until you get down to the kernel of truth, which is that I don't want to have my skin shaved off with a razor blade, layer by layer. It's the most immediate thing to my heart. It's the thing from which everything else proceeds.

Gina   That's what I like about you. You have no clue about truth, or art or beauty or meaning for that matter. But you are so solidly proud of *your* silly little rationalities, that it keeps me from confronting *my* utterly gorgeous and destructive visions of stark meaning. Keeps the wolf from the door, so to speak. Almost as though you know too much to really be normal. Like you are from the other side.

Kate   Eat the wolf, not me.

The two girls are sitting in the office lounge. They put their feet up on the coffee table and stretch their legs their smooth stockinged legs with the slippery shoes on the ends, and they admire their hipbones, how they are constructed, and they stroke down each others' thighs and Gina pulls out a knife. *Just let me trim your hair*, she says. *Let me trim the ends are split and that's not healthy girls cut their hair at least once a month.* Gina sighs happily. *As long as I can continue to surround myself with utter morons who do not get haircuts*, she thinks, *I will never have to face my destiny of confronting truth and telling it that it is a construct. Yet this is my goal.* Kate meanwhile probably gloating. Probably stroking her little fiendish images. Thinking she has thought. Thinking she has it all saved somewhere saved up as a brace against never knowing anything.

—Here is Gina (standing over with knife) Nice girl, kinda chubby, sweet face, no important blemishes or at least no visibly obvious horrible ones. She has nicely painted nails, soupy eyes, dreamy body coordination, and a clever little jaw.

—Here is Kate (spread out on the xerox machine) Gangly limbs, olive skin, hair everywhere, scared bright clown eyes open wide, no softness in the joints, only kind of waxy. Something you would pick at if not a person. OBVIOUSLY. A victim.

Gina slices through Kate's outers. If Kate had no nerve endings, or if they were markedly less sensitive, this would be an interesting and pleasurable experience for her. Gina chooses to imagine it in such a way, having taped shut the mouth and tied down the hands.

There now, she says, Look at that - a spiral down your lovely back.

Gina has Kate tied down on her stomach because honestly one more look at that revolting waxy picked-at bubbleheaded face would be too many. She slices down through the flesh covering the spinal cord, thinking per-haps that truth would be a cell in flux, travelling endlessly up and down the cord, pushing maybe some large rock which everlastingly rolled back down, like that one dude. She makes a few diagonal cuts across the spine, hoping to reveal truth flashing by in a hurry, or at least impede its progress, the sallow little sprite. But, when she has acheived absolute visibility, the spinal cord reads hollow and empty. Disappointing. Really. She makes a photocopy of her work. Nothing here. Stupid stuck-up hole.

Looking down she is reminded of another time. There was a child standing between the lanes at a streetlight, and he was really actually cute, and he was wanting money for some project or other, survival. The source of her power was the fact that she could look at him from her car and be harsh or sneering or kind or sweet or she could flip him off or smile warmly, see, it had nothing to do with HER situation. It had no direct affect on what would happen if SHE ever ended up in the middle of an intersection asking for change. That's what's good about the world being as big as it is. You don't have to deal. As another example, take vivisection. Were she to end up on the operating table, it is probable that the person with the knife would not be aware of how she had treated Kate, so if she were nice now, or if she were cruel, it would not hurt her future in the least. Comforting, when you're in the middle of something, to realize you're safe.

Gina hastily applies a wad of copy paper to the back, to staunch the flow of blood, and makes two incisions, starting at the back of each knee and tracing a curve through the inner thigh up into the pubic hair. Nothing running around down there. Only a thick meaningful muscle mass, and the parting skin becoming thin like paper, maybe the girl has died. Gina places her hands over the warm deep slices in Kate's thighs. Those slender thighs so unfed by hearty gruel. Gina becomes interested in science. What is beneath Kate's tender knees. She shaves away the skin layer by layer, revealing complex intricacies and delicate weavings of ligament, bone, structure, formal lines. It's beautiful down and in there. Gina realizes and makes a note that as long as you're not fat, you can always rest in the beauty of your inside tissue. Even a waxy clown has wonderful knees. Even a horrible goat has interesting connections between extremities and trunk.

UNNGHNGAAAAH sàys Kate. Gina presses print.

Gina turns Kate over and spreads the legs. This has become inevitble, since the hesitant exploration with her tongue, before, that early red tissue, found to be hot, found to be not sweet. It's NOT beautiful. It's not a thing to be explored. Ugly vital flesh. How could anyone steel themselves to push in there, let alone stay there. Even the furtive and embarrassed figure of Truth would scoff at such a portal. Not the right place to be a lady. Not the right venue for ladylike behavior. Gina slices off the outer pair, careful, careful. It looks even worse. She lays out the removed pieces on the glass and squashes Kate's pelvis down to get a better shot. Too bad it is black and white. Gina puts her finger into the hood and feels no response in the way Kate's jumping about, frigid bitch. She wasn't so frigid when truth was an abstract, able to be embraced with the abstract arms of faith. *Liar.* Gina jabs, thinking that the hurt of it will be deep and painful, unlike the other cutting things which did not imply a great violation. *This time it's for real*, Gina murmurs, *You're gonna give it up for me.* Gina turns and raises her naked bottom to the table. Do you want to see my bottom, *you FAGGOT?* she hollers. *Think you are so brave with no cunt lips now. Think you are so detached. I'll find you in there and you won't be able to hide under some desk or other because I've had them all carted away and there's just you and me and some knife.* Gina recalls many scenes from movies where an exorcism

45

is taking place and she thinks *this is a similar situation* except that she's been able to transcend her innately flawed desire to worship human life. *Look, I'm only a messenger*, says Gina, *Don't blame me.* And really, you're not supposed to blame the messenger. This is true.

As the excavation continues, Kate begins to heave in a heaving of desperation. She has to get off of that xerox machine but there is just no way. Tied. Gina presses her ear to the ribcage of the bloody mass. You have to finish the job once you start. If only things had been irrationally different, not complying with the expected ways of human physiology, rather switching to a more artistic mode. Wounds heal instantly, no blood flows, when you move on you move on and there's not any nasty scratching of the old openings against the marks that say 8.5x11, 11x17. Of all the sad words of tongue or penis, the saddest are these: "When you cut, it stays cut," and the victim isn't going to lie there enjoying it. Why can't you just make up things and have them be real? But the thing is, if the victim is dead, then it's not really vivisection. You have to keep the person alive, or else it's something else probably autopsy. Kind of a pointless autopsy, but certainly one that will be conclusive.

The sad truth is in the stomach, she decides. The stomach is shaped like a primitive horn cleverly opened at both ends, in and out. Slice. Truth cowers in a corner, sucking its own navel, and shaking. When it shakes, the beads it has tied into its hair rattle and make great noises. Truth is a pretty good dresser. FOR AN EXTINCT PILE OF SHIT!!! And the bitch wasn't faking. Go figure.

As Kate suffers and dies, Gina takes Truth into her hand lovingly. She is no longer afraid. How the other girls used to cower and run when it threatened to show through the web of evil that surrounds us all! How they had fainted to show how weak and unworthy! Silly girls. Darling little dead truth. Sighing and gasping in her hand. She squished it. The end.

Ricardo has a Line for Everything

they were investigating if she was an unfit mother because her husband had been killed so hideously, and then the investigators too got killed, god knows how. suspicion turns to the family itself, and if the family is to get away, they will have to drive all the pickup trucks they had lived in, and junior is five, and marta is thirteen. she will miss her boyfriend. the mother could hook up a tow line for one of the pickups but not the other. they will have to leave the old ford. dry hot wind blows over the desert while the three people stand around the old truck. *will the radio come out,* says marta. *no it's old,* says mother, *junior can come in my truck.* marta turns away sulking, her mouth bitter and sucking on itself. this infighting gives the enemy an edge. women with tits and bushes painted on their clothes who after all were called by rampant female mysticism out of their homey caves. coming over the desert to enslave them. bringing the forest with them. mother drapes a heavy chain over the axle and wraps it around itself twice before tying it to the other truck. it is hard to tie a chain. then they are ready for the great getaway.

JANE and MARTIN are the new investigators. of killings and other family dramatics. *here is the murder weapon,* says

JANE, holding up a meat tenderizing mallet made out of wood. *it seems so whole*, says MARTIN. she places it on the desk, squinting up her eyes willfully. *she covered him in bars of soap and put the mallet in a pillowcase*. it's obvious to her what happened. but martin could never figure out anything he is so dumb. MARTIN's hair is black and wet but it's only gel. JANE's hair is beautiful curly red and soft. she wears grey suits with short skirts, sexy. she has panty hose with seams, like everyone used to have. she is behind the times again. she picks up the murder weapon and waves it through the air, hot under her clothes, she makes designs against the wall in afternoon sunlight. she will finish this story within the hour, but time passes rapidly in the office, slowly out on the desert, when they are digging through the piles of belongings at the homestead, hoping that someone will stop them, come up and say *i know what's going on here, i know what you're doing and what you should do*. JANE's hands are jammed hard around the mallet's handle, both of them, *it's the children i'm thinking of* she says.

marta sits in the second truck with her hands beside her legs, getting pulled along by the tow chain. the seat is vinyl. perhaps if the boyfriend came running after her she could put all her weight on the brake or does it not work with the car in neutral. does the car just roll. the boyfriend could run, sweating and extending himself, his stomach tight and his thighs pounding next to each other opening and closing. she could roll down the window and stick out her hand and he could grab it and pick up his legs to rest them, get carried along over the road until he could run some more. it wouldn't take long for him to get his wind — she could hold him up for that amount of time. marta fluffs her hair in the rear view mirror. that morning she was in the creek with a bottle of dish soap. she rinsed everything clean. she put creek mud on her face and let it dry, looking in the eddy where her reflection was steady. marta sticks her hand out the window into the breeze and it might brush against the light foliage along the road's shoulder, scraping it. here, take hold and rest, good job. she can feel the grip on her arm maybe hurting, straining with the exertion of holding him. his legs swing dangerously close to the truck, he could be battered to death.

all over the world there are feminists in fact literally every-where. doing all these funky things. making up prayers and planting little fruit trees for the goddess. doing stupid things with tampons that nobody wants to hear about. summoning what. tapping what. making pretty pictures of some leaf woman and some druid type fantasy broad. oh nature. oh the earth mother. oh the power and beauty of my piss.

JANE and MARTIN are together. they are an item. he fixes her car, he changes the lining in her pool. all they can examine are the three fords. when they have watched the family walk out into the desert they make their move, speaking quietly and moving fast like they have been trained for years. *do you have to smoke while you are pregnant to hurt the baby?* says JANE or *can it be after or before, the same thing.* she picks up a white cigarette butt and puts it in her pocket, to be examined. *maybe it's the kid's cigarette* says MARTIN. JANE gives him the look of shut up because he is too dumb to understand words. MARTIN picks up a piece of broken wood and says *the murder weapon.* then they see some people or wolves coming and they want to scram as fast as possible. to preserve anonymity. *take this brother, may it serve you well,* he says, waving the wood toward some unseen person, then he is slashing with it, trying to prove that it could have been used to kill, that it could be dangerous, that it could hold malice in its grain, in the broken end that could stab.

down the road a hundred miles the family stops at a bar. mother spends time doing up her hair while junior fiddles with the dark tampon hanging from the rear view mirror. to prevent stealing. another one is on the battery, along with some razor blades carefully glued sticking straight up and hidden so they could cut a hand reaching in to steal. when the trucks were stopping the one in tow bumped into the other one's bumper so junior gets out to check the damage. he has fat knees and elbows, blonde curly hair, he is a child with lips red from koolaid. he drinks it straight out of the cooler spout because putting it in cups can make it hotter. he has a few red spots on his thighs from drippage. *bump you* he says to marta with his hand spread across a ding in the fender. marta is determined not to move out of the truck, so mother has to pull her by the hand into the bar and slam the door behind them angrily. marta smears her hair down flat, no one here will see how beautiful she is now, she cements it down with spit and leers at the waitress who tells them the soup is cream of cauliflower. *but it's separated* says the waitress, *you may not want to eat it.*

what do they want some primordial female presence coming in a swarm up out of the desert bringing with it foliage bringing with it lush power and of course since innocence is dry bringing a wet death? sure go be a witch and feel so connected and sing to the moon that nipple in the sky and think how absolutely untouched and how primitive the energy and then get your husband raped up the ass with a primitive energy fencepost and then slaughtered and you to blame. hot shit feminist you are now.

the people on the horizon have stopped coming and anyway maybe they were just trees growing up. look says MARTIN, *dirt which has been disturbed by someone digging in it.* he has had so many head injuries that he has patches of hair which stick up to mark the places. most of them are marked. he falls out of cars when they are moving, and sometimes when he is driving. it's not safe. the desert, then the forest. once JANE took him to get his ankle set at the charity hospital in town and there were cigarette butts, people screaming, syringes on the floor huddled in corner nooks, the man behind the curtain was having minor surgery with no anesthetic. *let's have a look at that hole* says JANE. they use the stick to paw through dirt until they see it *that there's five periods worth of tampons* says MARTIN. *can you not say that* she answers. *you know i ask for three things — you don't talk about bodily functions, you don't keep finishing every drink i open and every plate of food i set down, and you don't piss everywhere all over the place.* MARTIN keeps poking the tampons with a stick not looking at her. *you piss on the garden, you piss on the wall, i come out tired in the morning to find you pissing off the dock into the lake. now cover that shit.* MARTIN picks up an old cookie sheet and places it over the hole, thinking the sun will concentrate its heat here and the cancer will burn itself off the wall of the cervix. or the moon will concentrate its light. *what,* he says, *do you never fart? do the angels come and carry it away?*

mother's ratty summer dress looks good to junior. he puts his fingers in his mouth and stacks napkins on the bar, alternately grey, white, blue. it depends on which end is turned towards him. he rolls his eyes extravagantly at the waitress and she says *cutie-pie.* he is amusing himself. mother's soup comes and she lets him drink noisily off the side while she uses a spoon. marta doesn't want any soup. he calls her *fatty.* he thinks the words Wicked Little Boy which have been said to him recently. he thinks there is a dog outside. he thinks *i am hungry for more soup.* a man comes up to mother. he is thin and wearing stupid clothes. his hat buttons down on itself in the front and marta says *he has no lips.* he clears his throat and reads from a yellow pad of paper, legal sized. *my name is ricardo and i would like to get to know you better.* mother looks down at his back pockets stuffed with little pieces of paper. notes? receipts? mother says *what did you say* because ricardo has a very thick accent. *you are very beautiful a very beautiful woman* says ricardo, reading it. *um* says mother, *i can't go out with you anywhere. i'm wanted by the law.* ricardo pages through his tablet, looking for what she said and what to say back, but he can't find it. instead he smiles and says *i would like to get to know you better*, this time with better english sounds.

JANE and MARTIN have found the pond. they were beating through the new undergrowth which scratches and it opened up underneath them they fell in. as they moved toward each other they noticed the phosphorus algae in every little wave they made, glowing, getting doused and going under. dark fronds waved over their heads in the falling night and they felt cooler than ever, brushing up against each others arms and legs with their soft wet limbs, and MARTIN getting silly with his hands. even the third truck had been overtaken by it, vines in the windows and rusty holes. just as JANE gets down under the water some bubbles come up from behind by MARTIN's butt and she smacks at him, throwing her hair out of her face. *you shithead, can you not fucking do that?* martin shrugs and swims sedately to the other side, kicking his legs in rhythm and deep underwater and pushing his lips up above the surface by grimacing. he takes his shirt off to wring it dry and sits down on a cooler that is there. JANE pushes him off and opens it up, *it's a coleman,* then both of them smell the stinkiness. *pee is in there,* says MARTIN. they are peeing in there for a toilet. JANE points over to the strawberry patch in the clearing, *it's to keep the bugs and animals away from the berries.*

mother you freak — saw you peeing in a circle around the

group on the beach, squatting down every couple of feet saying something about territory then asking people to make swishy watery sounds because it helps the pee come never thinking there's the fucking ocean right there what do you need a vacuum hose up your snatch. and if it sounds violent it's only because oh the ruination. you meddling in your little chanting holiness and being sure everyone hears you saying my goddess instead of my god. wish the plant women brought their forest of death right down your throat instead of being such obedient little summoned demons swallowing up your sworn enemies oh dying men. not a bad husband you lost, hasty chanter. better think of where you draw the line friend foe and when you bring in recruits that won't understand the purpose of moderation.

ricardo can you drive a truck says mother. ricardo pulls some paper out of his back pocket and looks at it, then gives it to mother, who also looks at it. *never mind,* she says, *you can ride in with marta.* she and ricardo sit in the truck together getting pulled along by the tow chain and junior is in mother's truck with his face and hands pressed against the back window and his mouth sloppily open. *how are you doing today* says ricardo *well.* marta says *no* and does not look over, she straightens her dress out straight and wonders will we let him out at the town or will we keep him. *how are you doing today* says ricardo this time reading it slowly and then adding *well.* he does not smile or encourage her to answer by gesturing toward her, he keeps his head down and his butt sunken into the truck seat is thin and wan. a sad body thinks marta generously. she can imagine him moving into a house nearby where they used to live and driving up and mother would come out of one of the trucks with a pie she had baked to welcome him and the desert dust would blow over the pie and in her dark hair. he would be flattered she had made the pie. and father would have not yet been killed by the painted on women. and the desert would be dry sand no trees in sight. she can see that the thick green of many trees is meeting over the road now closing on itself knitting together dripping with soft clean water making pools in the road slapping at the sides of the trucks with spongy tender wide leaves. ricardo seems to hear it. he turns and points to the rear window and makes up a brand new sentence, *there it comes to us.*

the sound begins with birds and then becomes children and mothers. JANE and MARTIN have not done the job or answered the questions was the father killed by a mallet, can the mother stay in trucks and still keep children in school. as they clutch for each other's hands in the warm pond when the leaves come into the water dipping and diving, the leaves are reaching for them too, to get the hands first and keep them locked. stuck to the sides of the pool they struggle and hear the sounds of coming people. is it the family were they hiding safely in the transmissions or diluted into the strawberry pee or were they between tampons covering themselves with moss. MARTIN and JANE choose not to think that they are being held down by a forest. but when the women come in their white jumpsuits two round circles for breasts and black dots with raised paint for nips, one black triangle each between the hips messily painted on possibly in a hurry, these women have no trouble restraining the two investigators.

as the trucks have more and more difficulty plunging through the emerging woods signifying their approach oh the bounteous nature the lurching motion of the second truck speeding up and slowing down yanking on the tow chain makes the heads of marta and ricardo jerk back and forth. like they are nodding. it is their truck that gets a branch wrapped around the axle and such a strong branch that the tow chain breaks and ricardo gets his head knocked on the dash board for it. mother's got a line between the wrinkles on her forehead when she throws her truck into park and jumps out. *stay* she says to junior who leans far out the window. mother comes around to the driver's side where marta is with her foot on the brake. grabbing the girl's arm she throws her out of the truck and stretches in to ricardo's knocked out hand. it is hard to pull him out and his bag gets stuck on the seat belt lock. one pull she is sweaty now with him half out going to land on his head and she pulls out the papers leaving nothing in the truck and him in the side of the road smashed on his head with his neck uncomfortably twisted. he is knocked out still poor sacrificial ricardo. marta reaches for the bag of papers but her mother has a hand on the back of her neck to guide her angrily to the truck that works. already the leaves are scratching at ricardo's clothes they have turned him over flat on the dirt and bound him up tight the women are coming from ahead on the path that was a road. marta finds herself climbing in the truck wanting to see what happens to ricardo, and her mother, being left alone by the women, is untangling the tow chain. when they are all in the truck and driving it is through the hordes of women with painted on tits and bushes who have been coming from ahead, and they all step out without any screaming and mother is sweating gripping the wheel and junior is looking at the thin green juice on his hand from fighting off the tree. in one quarter mile the forest has been crumbling down into sand dry sand and by the side of the concrete road there is nothing but little pieces of trash and paper and junior presses his face against the back window wondering what do those women like to eat and wondering if we drive slow will they come back.

Master Assassin

As soon as Sabrina had decided that she was definitely infertile, she realized she was already six months pregnant. As soon as Clive decided Sabrina wasn't kidding, she'd split town.

Dear Clive,
Isn't it just so incredibly fascinating? Who would have thought that sex was actually viable? But this way, you'll be able to succeed and all. The most important thing is that nobody resents anyone.
Love, Sabrina

Well, actually, the resentment was fairly intense. And Clive was thrown entirely off his game. The very next time he stuck out his hand to greet someone, he saw a thick curly horrible hair growing out of his palm. He jerked his hand back into his pocket and explored the interior of his fist with his middle finger. No hair. He pulled his hand out of his pocket. Hair. The man he was trying to greet stared at him kindly and offered him a mint. Clive took this to mean give me a closer look at that hairy palm. No thanks he said. But you asked for one, said the man.

The most grievous thing was that they had been so in love. Real love the kind that makes you crazy to get home from work. He knew most decidedly that she was still in love with him. Had she not just the day before said so repeatedly? and now gone? He was oh so eternally sad. Intense sadness filled him. He felt sadder (he imagined) than a deep dark cave at the bottom of a hole that would never know sunlight. He felt in short really fucking sad. Her cat name of Becky had stayed behind. Apparently on a melodramatic flight from domesticity, you don't need any aimless old cats dragging along. He fed it, bathed it, held it, and renamed it Bik Yee. He found comfort in words that are pronounced in a similar way, yet have different spellings. Felt that some fluctuation was possible in the universe. Felt that pregnant girlfriends who have sworn to you that you will be eternally free of their troubles and needs may at once come bouncing back all needy to trouble you excessively.

He wrote to her, long letters. You are not an elephant head he said. You do not have to go away and die. Then he tried the it's-my-baby-too approach but he knew that one wouldn't work, what with all the my body my temple crap she used to read in college. Clive was a young scientist. But suddenly, he couldn't even talk to Sabrina. And they had had such fun together. I'll love you even if you go away and raise up my child to be a master assassin he used to joke with her before it actually happened. Is it really proper or advisory to joke about the future well the *possible* future of a relationship in which one is currently engaged? Is engaged in retrospect really an inappropriate word choice?

The pregnant woman flees habitually to one of the poles - north or south. Polarities are immutable at such locations. Light, dark. He loves me, he loves me not. Pregnancies are immutable in most locations. Pregnant or not pregnant. Dead, or not dead. So he wondered, which pole? He had always thought, before all this, that her mathematical interest in numbers, equations, and their absolute proofs, had been cute. Cutie, he had said. A mathematician himself however, he now found her blatant disregard for error, probability, chance, and random pagan rituals to be irritating and tragic. He found himself chanting sentences that began with "the love they had shared was..." such as ending it with "never to be realized" or "beyond death" even though these sentiments were not only melodramatic but also inapplicable. He didn't care. Sitting in his dining room chair, the one with the arms, and there were only two, he brooded and fussed with the lighting to make it just possible that one of the shadows was actually Sabrina playing a clever trick. People find this sort of behavior nauseating in a man. He was missing a lot of information. Where was she, first on the list. Why did she leave, second. Is she okay, third. You see. Not even a missing link more of a missing chain.

Sabrina sat at her desk as a part-time receptionist in Houston where she had moved. She answered the phone promptly, opened no one's confidential mail, invented cute office sayings, ingratiated herself with all the vice presidents, never interrupted the president on the phone, and was soon promoted to head office of the corporation in an unprecedented back to back promotion hailstorm and eventually led the entire company from a comfortable home office and now living in the Heights she resided peacefully with her newborn child. She named the child Bismark because it sounded European and everyone knows that Europeans are completely ruthless.

On her way into the city for burritos in the dark of night Sabrina would look up from driving and see next to the tallest building her work building with an ice castle (she called it) on top. The entire top floors ornamentally lit from the inside in turrets and in the center a square and in the square outlined in blacked out windows she saw very clearly from miles away the outline of a woman's face and shoulders. Which was a very proud woman. An honor to be put up there on the ice castle certainly, a beacon to those who as Sabrina, had purchased their CEO letterhead with whatever, whatever, and even though pregnant had looked Happy in the face and said grandly and nobly Give me Dignity. Sabrina thought Dignity was a rather splendid name for a child although if a girl the obvious porn career, Hot Dignity Dog, made it a bad choice. OH Sabrina was proud and OH she was absolutely and constantly pissed. To think of the curly yards of lace! To think of the slaving and festering under disowned luggage and jewelry as presents at every anniversary!

When the child was born it surprised everyone by being

fifteen years old within three days. She, the Bismark, sucked on pablum anyway, and staring at her finger in front of her face would think "expressionless" and think "invisible" and think "awake." She read almost everything historical. Considering herself a depository. She fucked like a dog with a knot in its dick and clamped tight afterwards to the scared skinny phantasms for sometimes an hour not letting them slink away retreat she was absolutely infertile her mother saw to it. She is not a violent person, her mother would say. For example. Keeps her room very clean never knocks anything over. For another example. Did not participate in blood sports when offered the chance. Never took martial arts. Never raises too much of a stink. Never fights. Just wins. Are you SCARED YET? are you SCARED YET MR. CLIVE DOCTOR MAN? Because she is scary, scary. The kind of girl you don't want to come after you in a blood rage so quiet and still and straight-haired that you almost don't recognize yourself and the woman you spent years mooning over blended with genetic certainty into an awesome killing machine.

But nobody recognized or agreed that the only way to really have a child in these struggling earnest love relationships is to run away and be awful. What else are you going to do? Sacrifice? There's not the time. But still, either way, it stinks.

For Clive, the hallucinations have now ended. No more hairpalm no more greasy pens that won't let him hold onto them just slip through only they don't it's just him not

63

holding hard enough though he thinks he's holding very hard indeed. No more singing drearily about love and her. After a year of solid spermophobia, Clive had almost forgotten that he had genitals, let alone the fact that at one point he had plunged his penis full of zooming zinging sperm into a then receptionist now world power mother of death. Clive was content with his work, figuring out little engineering problems for minor companies who manufactured audio equipment. More like keeping up really than plunging ahead. The one shock of his life, Sabrina's disappearance, had become "then" and this was happily "now."

Sabrina was a lifestyle he thought, she thought. Clive could remember the minute that he consciously rationally decided to change his life forever by jumping into her car and being driven god knows where every damn day for the rest of his life. Except that she stopped at a gas station, jumped out to get cigarettes, and took off running down the road. Him in the car, stuck. Her bitterly staring back at him as he did not follow. Her carrying Bismark under her arm like a gun, waiting to use her on him. Which he did not know was there. Which he never knew was his problem. She had told him it was NOT his problem. Had told him go away and I will go away and we will never trouble you again, eyes daggers. She (never realizing, one day, totally dead phones) had lied. There she was all the while smiling as mournfully as any brave martyr, promising secretly to trouble him endlessly murderously when the two females turned strong and brisk and wealthy and the poor gentleman doctor aged drastically by manufactured grief to be rather frail actually no match. She, the Bismark, the girl barbarian hunted him and hounded him for months, dragging it out not out of pity but out of a desire to relish this her life's mission.

The doctor took to the woods. Once alarmed his nervous guilt was freakishly sensitive. He had simply nothing to say to this child. What she must have been TOLD about him the LIES the terrible slander how he had cried over her mother and her and how everything was could have been would be different onward came the glitter eyed Bismark, avenger of mislaid babies and girlfriends not safely wed to kill him with her own cold weapons of hate. He hid. Developed an accent half British half Indian barely recognizable from his old half drawl. He crouched under a desk in the middle of a freight yard breathing low and keeping his shoes up off the ground hoping not to be heard. Bismark entered the freight yard silencing the guard dogs with one hand she was very whateverosensitive that thing that means when you can talk to animals almost telepathic with them there is no level of mysticism and no strange haunting quality denied this character. She is not only pale but also very fragile. Yet strong as bullets. She is daunting perhaps the most daunting yet. Fucking your father is called incest. Murdering your father is called patricide. But is he really her father. Can he not be because she is vile and loathsome and strictly dominant. Nothing pretty about her not even her eyes can be said to be tender. Perhaps not even to the touch. Perhaps hard.

Clive the doctor huddled safely under the desk in the freight yard clutching the cat Bik Yee. To him the cat meant, Look I changed my name. I used to be only Becky but now I am Bik Yee. I can't drive a car. I can't even sniff a train. I'd die. But I can change my name and all the old things I had to answer to like Becky come Becky stop destroying drapes, those things no longer apply. I can stamp them with a mighty stamp of Not Me. Perhaps, at the end of his long exile of months, he would turn and face his daughter and make a big show of being nice to the cat. Perhaps he would lift up the cat and stroke it and pet it and make idiotic crooning noises to it and sing perhaps and one of two things. She would think crazy or she would think nice. You can't kill either one of those. He was kind of sad to be so desperate because in the old days of loving Sabrina he would have braved a thousand homicidal maniacs before breakfast but now he was saddened and sicked. So sad. So sick. Him sick and sad. Precious baby darling Bismark would see and understand nothing. She was a Master Assassin <theme music> and she blasted his ass into shit right there under the desk.

Sabrina was upset. Everyone was. No one had known that he would have kept the cat with him though vaguely allergic or that the cat would have stayed, though it never favored him when there were choices. Sabrina took it as a tremendous sign of his eternal devotion to her and decided to rethink the way she had treated him and that everything didn't have to be so black and white and she could have just thought about things for a second, been reasonable, breathed, but then she looked at her beautiful murdering daughter all straight wholesomely bloody picking through the remains of her father, and she thought, no, if I'd settled down and had china and we'd struggled and made it and raised her and happily jogged along to this, we'd never have had this kind of imagery.

Uncle George and the Roofers

Dianna was getting the band back together, only this time, as roofers. She picked up Hazel, picked up Slaveboy, drove for three days. *Rock 'n' Roll aside,* she said, *I'm going to find my amazing country paradise farmstyle habitation, mansion, dreamland.* She pointed out selections from the countryside including watery dams and several old oaks. Hazel rode in the back and the roofing equipment was not an easy seat for her. Yet it seemed peaceful and right for them to be together.

Look at her, said Slaveboy. *all mashed against the tar paint brush. You can't believe in her and not believe in her death and disfigurement. You can't defile her and not defile every young roofer with a talc smudge under each tenderly shaped eye.*

Slaveboy had the wheel and Dianna was pointing out the sights in her old neighborhood where she had been young and a child. *Look there is where the crazy old janitor turned out to be a pervert. Look there is where the fire burned down the old grange which was just used for nothing anyway.* Hazel mostly shifted in the back seat. The day was humid and difficult. Everyone hated hearing the monologue. What did she know anyway? with her ragged hair. Insurrection. Drama. The desire to Rock Out. Ten miles later Dianna was out of the car and crunched up against the curb, her skinny legs and arms bound around her body like twine. She was slack, and deadly. Rubber sneakers, rubber mini-skirt, rubber bra. Nothing was tight enough to fit her. Her BONES were too small. Everyone LOVED her. *I'm going to give you a lesson,* she said to her mutts sitting in the street. They crunched up their bodies, imitating her style, as if they could do it. They had to use gel to achieve that hair effect. Hazel was particularly pretty. Hateful slut. Gruesome girl.

I'm not playing the guitar any more said Dianna sitting there in the gutter. *This is what I mean. Now instead of that which you should have hoped to find during the slam sessions, you shall now find in the occupation of roofing. And although the only fun part is ripping up the old roof, you shall not stop at this. And no balking. No hopefulness. No tears.*

Instead of repainting the truck to have some more professional logo they left the name of it "Slags" and just put the word "Roofers" underneath it in almost the same color paint. When they started up again Dianna sat proudly in the back throwing sound equipment out over the highway to make room for the extra supplies they would need. So they travelled and travelled and had many adventures and at last they came back to the country of Clarion in Pennsylvania. They had a client. The client was Auntie. She had answered the radio ad. Auntie wanted her roof redone. They went to see her.

Auntie was NICE. Auntie was NICE and SWEET and KIND. Auntie had treats for nice doggies that behaved, so everyone was a nice nice little doggie, even Dianna. By day the roofers climbed ladders and raked their hands through the rotted tar paper and gouged themselves with nails and fought with gnats and drank soda and beer. By night the revelries in the back of the pickup were loud under the pines. Auntie found the whole thing charming.

Look, biddytits she said to Dianna rashly, *move over your little butt and gimme gimme.*

Auntie probably had been born in 1913. She had that look about her. Even Dianna found her to be measurably pleasant. The orange cinderblock house was certainly uninspiring enough with its square roof and two storeys. Good thing they didn't have to roof the tower. It was three storeys. GOOD THING THEY DIDN'T HAVE TO ROOF THAT TOWER. WHEW!

Hazel turned out to be very good with rope, and she said that it was fun for her to tie the ropes to the top of the roof and then around the waists of the more active participants (Dianna and Slaveboy). No one wanted to fall down off the roof. Yet it seemed that someone inevitably would, since they were so fucked up all the time. As it turned out, Auntie caused it. It was not their fault.

CHILDREN she came shrieking out of the house on a Sunday. *YOU ARE ALL MY CHILDREN.* Slaveboy may have been playing around or maybe just fed up with it, but he came crashing down onto his bottom in an inglorious heap. He was probably broken. They hauled him into the truck and set him up with an ashtray and a portable tv. From then on his job became roofing consultant. Not that he came up with any good ideas. Just that he talked about his pain a lot, and called it his office.

With Slaveboy out of commission, the roofing process took a decided change for the worse. It's not like Dianna didn't know how to put on a roof. It's very simple. Take off the old roof, put on the new roof. Make sure it stays on by applying some sort of fixative. But she struggled with the tar paper rolls and found herself humming old Slags tunes and thinking about her mother or family. It is sad to be alone up on the roof. It makes you pensive. Hazel became roof decoration. It stank.

One brisk fall day a car pulled in. Auntie piled out of the house singing *CHILDREN YOU ARE ALL MY CHILDREN* and embraced the sagging people who had come. One woman. One man. Both whiny and trite. Dianna scoffed at them under her uncomfortable tar mask. She had a paintbrush in one hand and sent it flying through the air dripping wet tar and creosote and attracting bugs and flecks of crap from the air. It landed in the hair of that woman. Her pile of crisp curls all up and lifted and free got stuck in that whorey brush and plied one from the other in a mess of black and sticky tar.

What, is this roofing an all day project? said the woman stickily. *Don't you ever go home? Don't you ever finish.*

Let's just say that the job offers aren't exactly rolling in, and I want to suck this stupid granny mother porcelain doll for all the pension she's worth, Dianna spat back.

Look at Dianna. She's greasy. I hate her, said the man. *I mean she's just awful. She's dirty. There's one room where she dumps her garbage and it smells. The workmanship is hideous. There is a little section of a living room closed off for the children and she sets up a table in the living room and that's what she has. There's one room for the toilet and one room for the people. Which actually was very convenient, because when WE were staying there, there were six of us. In Dianna, hot water is centrally provided. When Dianna turns off hot water, it's off. Well we were on the fourth floor. We had this little pail, and we had a bowl.*

I'd fill up the pail with a little hot water from the bowl, and then a little cold, and then pour it on myself. One person that was with us, well he probably just took cold showers (polite laughter). *Our job is to come back and let our people know what help can be given to Dianna and what help will be accepted. There is no method of transport southeast. There is no traffic. There's no lines for lanes in the road. And when the traffic is blocked going your way well you just kind of go into the other lane* (polite laughter). *But she is of course a native and really sweet and nice.*

Dianna looked around.

WHAT the fuck is this some kind of bloody fucking slide show conference report? I KNOW YOUR TYPE you half hybridized visit once a month fucking whore on your arm son. WHAT IS WITH YOU make me sick with your imperial bald spot I never saw someone before that I wouldn't let Hazel fuck but now I have.

Auntie raised a finger to the sky and reported from her investigation that the wind was up and she was going into town to change her will. AND THEN DIED. LEAVING DIANNA EVERYTHING.

Soon the police had finished with their questioning. They went home to their families leaving Dianna and her two people in the cinderblock house so far back from the road and with the tower and with the lawn and still had their truck and thinking they were settled now. The neighbors resolved loudly in public places that those people in Auntie's house would most certainly never be forgiven. Never let attend the fair. Never let achieve nuclear family status. And if in the future there were children or if that waify pretty girl were in fact now of age they would be denied 4-H membership or IF they were allowed to come then they would be kicked by younger members sitting on the shoulders of older members, their legs being operated like machines by the older girls. Murderers all three.

In the cinder house domestic duties were distributed. Dianna had the best room and collected rubber from roadsides to paper it and for the carpet which was just random on the floor not exactly nailed down. She liked her little room. It did not seem to her that she had killed the Auntie mother figure. It seemed on the other hand that this new house to live in and an entire countryside as an added gift was just perfect. She gained confidence. She gained body in her hair. She began to fill out to the point that she didn't bruise her butt just from sitting down on her bones. But see, you can't just inherit things especially relatives. You can't just walk in being the gardener or a stranger from the train and find yourself in possession of possessions. There are always people, and most things dribble down in sort of a linear fashion.

It seemed to be Hazel who was doing the most thinking. Dianna was beginning a little woodpile, preparing for winter. Slaveboy was an invalid, stuck up in the side room in bed with his mound of trashy novels and his secret play makeup. Everyone was FED. Everyone was HOUSED. But Hazel yearned for love.

LOOKIN' FOR LOVE in all the wrong places LOOKIN' FOR LOVE in too many ugly orange painted cinderblock towers with bad roofs. Hazel crept around the tower. Hazel scaled the wall of it, nearly to the first floor where the ceiling would be. Hazel sat nonchalantly on the metal fire escape type stairs that raggedly zagged up the side of the tower and smoked cigarettes, looking up, down, around, never INTO her own face, never letting the smoke waft directly up past any window. *WHAT IS IN THAT GODDAMN TOWER* she finally screamed at Dianna with wild eyes and hands flying madly from genitals to temples to amber waves of hair. Dianna stood there in the room, tossing squares of tire rubber onto the floor in different patterns, calmly evaluating them on a square by square basis. *You stupid fucking twat,* she said affectionately, *Get your moccasins. We're going in. I knew you wouldn't be able to restrain your knotted cunt forever.*

On the way downstairs they did the catechism beginning with IF the girl who said she was really going to dump her boyfriend was then heard later on saying "I LOVE YOU" to someone on the phone then what was the most likely assumption? NOT that she had taken him back. PERHAPS that she had never dumped him in the first place, using it only for drama and continued eyes on her bloated head. Hazel's education was a constant commitment. They circled the tower before beating the outside door down with their hands. *UP UP UP* they shouted and plunged heroically around the ascending spiral staircase inside to the top where the door was locked and an inside thought came out and said *maybe not so good.*

Dianna appeared as a specter of crusading, tight, vicious, one arm up and one pressed to side, her black skirt gripping on her legs and her trendy little shoes slippery and clipping on the stairs. Hazel oozed more like clouds do, tremulous and sweet. She did not appear as a flashing blur or a dark streak, but rather as an image here and then an image further on and then one further still, without the intermediate steps. She was wafting in her honey hair, while Dianna curtly chopped through her severed bangs, mod spod hot to trot little clot of hard cleavage. WHICH ONE to choose?

Behind the door lay stink. Really bad stink. So bad that they almost abandoned the project altogether. They swung the door open side by side, leaned in, leaned back out without moving their feet and swung the door shut. *Fuck,* said Dianna, *that's a rotten bad odor. We need cleaning materials,* said Hazel. *No* said Dianna. *We need to kill whatever's at the base of it.* Every odor has an equal and opposite death that stops it from stinking. *That doesn't make any sense* said Hazel.

Uncle George: GIRLS GET BACK IN HERE

The girls opened the door back up and there he was pile of flesh and skin waddling and pushing himself around with hands like forks. He was mostly skin and some mouth. The thing was, with all this skin, that he was rather wasted and thin.

Uncle George: HAVE YOU KILLED HER?

The girls felt a little silly, truth be told. Who could this pile of empty flesh hope to be but Auntie's diseased old nag?

Hazel: Sir, are you a horse?

Dianna: Never mind. We'll set you up with a nice little apartment downtown.

Uncle George: HAVE YOU KILLED HER?

Hazel: Who will clean him? He's filthy with dirt. Come on.

Dianna: I'll have to decide. I'll put it all in order. I'll fix everything up all nice.

A hand or tentacle or laser wand came out of the pile

that was him. It crept on the floor to Hazel and pushed itself at her feet.

Uncle George: You will be my special dragon slayer. Dear little girl who no one understands. I will help you to clean my skin. Bring a towel. I pick you. I choose you. My daughter. Pretty.

Dianna nodded sourly at last and left them to it. *Goodbye* she said. *Goodbye you sick little prat.* She continued her leave-me-out-of-it routine for many days. Hazel trundled back and forth to the tower with soap, shampoo, towels, buckets, small plates of salad, toothpaste, shaving cream, it all. Finally she tossed Slaveboy over her shoulder and announced to Dianna that a visit would be made to the tower to check on her really decent progress with Uncle George. *How is he* Slaveboy began in a whisper, *does he shove his fatted flank into your haunch when you bend to stroke his forehead with the damp towel. DOES HE PRONG YOU??? LITTLE SISTER?????* Slaveboy was apt to become hysterical at times, and everyone agreed that if his fall from the roof had in fact been intentional, that he had been sufficiently punished. For after all the roofing project was almost completed. And where was he with his injury? Stuck for life!

Hazel was wearing her presenting clothes. She looked just grand. She stood by the door at the top of the circular stairs inside the tower, flower in hair, microphone in hand. Her other hand was on the door, ready to fling it open at the appropriate moment.

Hazel's Speech:

I give you — a man deflated. I give you — a man in stasis. Perplexed, hardly moving, a tired man. I present to you the body of a man who was once so huge as to swallow the sea. Now so flattened as if a meteor had come crashing down on him from heaven, a squashed man. He has bones, doesn't he? He has arteries and distinct internal organs. His parts fulfill their functions in the whole. He has human statistics, pulse, breathing rate, desire for penile implants. (at this point she begins to worry that her hair is falling out because of weight loss during this project, she touches her ponytail at intervals, thinking "is this the size it used to be") I give you a man who once was wed, whose groin surged with pride and pleasure around the fecundity of a young wife. Whose wife becoming old chose to die at the hands of strangers leaving him this mystery, why did she never love him, why did she bury him in a specially crafted tower to wither and crumble nigh unto death itself. This mystery my friends has come to represent the life blood being force of the man that we call, lovingly, respectfully, hopefully, and generously UNCLE GEORGE.

Slaveboy and Dianna politely clapped. Dianna laid her hand on Hazel's head and said *This is all the hair you will ever have. You don't hear of people's hair getting thicker after all. Only thinner. And when you chose that particular brush and felt it ripping though maybe too hard and thought No, it's an expensive brush, it can't be ruining my hair, and when you chose that particular shampoo and never gave a thought to the fact that it might make your hair fall out, after all it's on the shelf with the rest of the shampoo, you were in actuality causing your hair to be dead.*

She put her hand around Hazel's hair and pulled off the ponytail holder. *There, put your hand around that,* she said Hazel did, hesitantly. *That hair used to fill up a fist. Now feel the limp slackness of your limb. Feeble, really. Hardly any hair there at all and what there is resembles khaki but silky in texture. Hair like a cat only not as dense. I hate your hair. Now you can show us your stupid scene and man, deflated girl, having no hair to show.*

Hazel peered at her dimly through her lovely greengoldbluedarling eyes. *You do* she said and ran away down the tower and out the door clinging to her remnants of hair.

Dianna dumped Slaveboy onto his feet and dragged him through the door.

Uncle George was dimly lit. His horror-grooves pervaded all through his skin, stretch marks, grease spots, bulges and recesses. He glowed with scrubbing. He was clean, CLEAN. There was no evidence of a bad dream or memories of walking. He seemed purged of his lowly agenda. His upper torso was propped on a pillow which had been carefully woven and then embroidered to resemble a fall of glorious blonde hair. His head of course was by nature shorn. There was a false radiance about him. Eerie. Dianna shivered. The room had been hung fabulously with glimmering robes and shifting curtains, beaded drapes and crystalline showers of fake jewels and gold nodules. Uncle George, had he been the King of Siam, would have opened his arms in stiff greeting and they would have been awed. Potentially even wed. As it was, he grunted to them and rolled his head from one side to the other creating ripples in the skin flaps and piles of bone-covering. NOT. AT ALL. PLEASANT.

Hey Slaveboy, said Dianna, *What do you bet I could get for this pile of rot if I set him out on the curb?* Slaveboy looked embarrassed. Perhaps Dianna would set HIM out on the curb one of these days and take five dollars or just the convenience of not having him around for someone to haul him away. They stick pins in you. Needles. They develop cures and you're the one that gets the PLACEBO. *OH fuck-all* she said. *You slimy worms can live up here and try to bond, if you're so bent on it.*

She stomped off down the stairs and left the two invalids in the royal tower to stew on each other. They shook hands. They invented lingo. They planned to go worldwide. Downstairs Dianna set up an office. It's more efficient to work in an office. It helps you concentrate and you can wear different clothes there than you do in the house. Also as an added benefit there is the trip from the office to the house, which is short enough to be untiring, but long enough to smoke half a cigarette. It was a good idea for a nice project and she gave Hazel the job of decorating it, mentioning firmly that she did not want it to look like a fucking b-movie persia. Hazel came through with a tasteful mauve and grey.

Projects can usually be distinguished from each other by notation of what paint was needed to accompany them.

For example, you can go into your basement and say There is the black and yellow paint that we used to paint those sets. Or you could point out the spray cans of purple and varnish that were used to restore the bookshelves in the nursery. Dianna separated one part of her office to be a workspace, and with one inch brushes and large sheets of white posterboard created five rummage sale posters. On the posters were images of fire (eyecatching), the address (country paradise), and a list of items to be sold.

LARGE ITEMS
- Black Couch with Footstool
- Tractor Mower
- Uncle George
- Slaveboy
- Post Hole Digger

SMALL ITEMS
- Vacuum needs work
- Garden hose, 50 feet
- Size 14 clothes, many
- Big Shot camera
- Indoor fig tree

Dianna put the posters in the local supermarket, gas station, the post office, the church foyer, and the tavern, hanging them amid cries of derision and scorn. They still hated her and called her murderer and thought she was evil, but she was undaunted. She knew that she had good wares and someone would want that post hold digger and would be necessarily present at her rummage sale and therefore would be on her property, therefore a visitor, therefore a guest.

Plenty of people came. It was a glorious festival day. Dianna thought of renting a pony or perhaps setting up a marquee with drinks on ice and berries with clotted cream.

Mostly people bought the other things but waited around silently hoping to witness what they apparently perceived as a white slave trade about to happen.

What's Uncle George is that a toy asked a child.

No, he's a disgusting old man, Dianna replied.

Hazel worked the money and exchange of goods. Dianna prowled around making sure nobody stole anything without paying. With the arrival of Auntie's real children came the complete unlawful chaos that everyone had been hoping for. Both children were stern and brushed down. They wore conservative clothes. They were accompanied by their own children. They were bad looking. Dianna stepped to them.

Look she said *I have swindled your inheritance, murdered your mother, moved into your birthplace and ridiculed your clothes. I now intend to make you purchase your father at an exorbitant price although god knows you'll regret it when you get him home.*

The insults began in an undertone coming from both at once like a stereophonic death chamber and Dianna stood firm in between them as they began to mutter then shout then holler.

His	Hers
you frothing whore i hate you make me sicker than this i have never been so angry as this is my finger in your steaming shit and wiping it brown on your hair reminds me	i still have a headache from last time. that creosote. my mother. my daddy. killing him would have been a nice thing for a sunday afternoon you slut don't you think that people

of cup up trash all shredded and stuffed back TOGETHER WE CAME HERE TO KILL YOU AND WE WILL BECAUSE KILLING YOU ARE **THE MOST UN- GRACIOUS HOST EVER IN THE HISTORY OF PARTIES** have relatives do you think YOU CAN JUST RANDOMLY EXECUTE PEOPLE OR SELL THEM OR ARE YOU **COM- PLETELY CRAZY IN YOUR HEAD THERE ARE ROCKS ROCKS ROCKS ROCKS ROCKS**

And this all at once strewn all over the lawn. Dianna picked up the bits of rant and scream, and put them up in jars to be used later possibly to make wine. Then she smiled at the nice respectable families who were standing there agape. *They won't even give me five dollars for their own father* she reported. *Not even five dollars* in her most sepulchral tones. The bidding began.

The very saddest thing of the whole day was that no one bought Slaveboy. It was okay though because he had enough bitterness in him to sour a thousand days. Uncle George's son won the race to see who could get to the highest sum without passing out from the knowledge that he was bidding on his own loin of origin. When Hazel did the math she figured out that they had grossed about $100,000 on the day's sales. They decided to turn the tower into an observatory.

The end.

⑨ *LINES AND SLOPE*

Chapter Nine Objectives

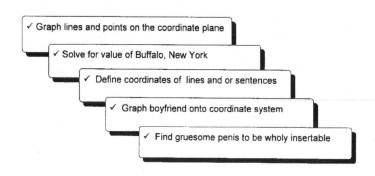

- ✓ Graph lines and points on the coordinate plane
- ✓ Solve for value of Buffalo, New York
- ✓ Define coordinates of lines and or sentences
- ✓ Graph boyfriend onto coordinate system
- ✓ Find gruesome penis to be wholy insertable

CHAPTER SUMMARY

Since there have been men and women there have been wives and mistresses. There have been women who were promised things, and women who received the benefits of things promised to others. A wife is a woman who can be trusted with keys, who can listen for hours, whose breasts can be fondled and kissed but not chewed. A mistress is a woman who is unaware of all that shit. She can get laid pretty easily. Men can choose each time whether to believe that their wives and their mistresses could be combined into the same person or not. Whichever they decide, they are not being honest. But they have to fuck their wives, unless they want to bear children in a fan out, with mistresses. It would be cool, if they could arrange this. It would be hard. People expect something more linear. It is expected that a man transform his wife each night into something which has nothing to do with her, and as far as the woman goes, she is not really responsible for what can happen.

PRETEST

The hair dye has marked out the scars in her hands, infecting them, leaving her with not even an intimate moment for the time when she was dying his hair.

1. "I don't want it totally red" he said.

2. "Anything is better than wearing a rainbow on your head" she said.

3. "There is nothing good to read in the paper" said his friend.

ANS: Across the table, with her hands in the sticky hair,

she stared at the friend. The shortest distance between two points is a line. The shortest distance between three points is not likely to be a line. It is not known what that would be. Two lines. Or, if three points on the same line, then, a line. The shortest distance between two points is a line, so those two points can move relatively easily along that line, to each other and away, having intimate moments, or being separated by two doors but still on the same floor of the same building. But points cannot jump over each other and change position. So her choices are as follows: she can move to the center of the table and say "Is there anything about this in the paper" (logical sequence of reply and response), she can go and stand on the other side of the friend and say "I thought socialists would read anything" (logical sequence of verb tenses past present subjunctive, symbolic resolution of the color term), she can stand directly behind the boyfriend and ask "What color would you like?" (logical sequence of reply and response). This final gesture seemed best, because it projected the friend so far down along the number line, logically, that he approached infinity. Still the moment was ruined.

9.1 *Sentences*

The RECTANGULAR COORDINATE SYSTEM is composed of four quadrants separated by two lines which cross. There are also lines which can be made into four lines, or which can be combined into one line. The shortest distance between two points is a line. The word "a" is singular. A line has no width and no breadth and is simple and good. When reduction is posssible, then also elimination is possible, and if elimination then relief.

EX: There are four lines with her. No one ever actually said them, or made them up. They are with her, in there, and they come up occasionally. It annoys her.

1. YOU SCUMBAG YOU MAGGOT YOU CHEAP LOUSY FAGGOT
2. THERE IS A REASON HE HASN'T BEEN AROUND IN A WEEK
3. SHE CHOSE THE WRONG CITY TO LIVE IN AND DIED THERE
4. I AM THAT SUPERBEING YOU HAVE NEVER YET DETECTED

The order or numbering, whichever she might impose, is irrelevant. They don't follow that, or never predictably. For example, the same one could come up three times in succession. Or she could almost forget it.

Figure 9.1 Boyfriend Graph

youscumbagyoumaggotyoucheaplousyfaggotthereisareaonhehasn'tbeenaroundinaweek

9.2 THINGS

An invention which would be worthwhile would be a sort of ironing tool that was a solid box with a tiny hole through the center. A pipette is a small glass tube used in chemistry. It is such a tiny tube that the exactness of it pulls liquids into it in small amounts, making these liquids into little lines instead of a mess. You just put the tube against the liquid and it gets pulled through in a line of near molecular width. The trick would be to get the hole in the solid box much thinner, so the pull would be much denser, and you could press an object against one opening, like a hair brush or a bag of chips, and on the other side it would come shooting out as a thin tight line which could be wrapped in a skein or let fall out the window as the car was driving away down the road to Buffalo. This would be a truly worthwhile invention.

EX. She wakes up in Detroit with a cat on her bed. "I am the superbeing you have never yet detected." He is sleeping in the other bed in the room, and the beds are lined up next to each other like an old couple would line up their separate beds.

1. Place and Vector: She doesn't really appreciate making this overnight stop, although she is tired. Now, instead of being at the surging endpoint of a vector headed for Buffalo, she feels like they are at the endpoint of a line segment that stops in Detroit. This is a familiar feeling, like when she is sleeping in her mother's bed in Detroit about five miles northeast, aware of the line segment that connects her to their apartment in Chicago. She had never before realized that there was a line segment connecting her to Buffalo as well. Maybe these things only become apparent with time.

2. Quilt and Cat: She dumps the cat hastily off the bed and picks up the quilt in her hands. "There is a reason he hasn't been around in a week." With her left hand pulling the edge through her right hand she closes her eyes and when she has come almost back around to the first corner she looks at the realigned quilt. The only dark part is the edge anyway. The middle is all triangles and patterned cloth. She simply doesn't have time. In a way, being in a different house like this (the friend's parents' house) is disturbing to her, because it is so surprising and unresolved. Also there are too many cats to figure out which one is which one's mother, and the genealogical charting. But in another way, it is better to move around. "She chose the wrong city to live in and died there."

3. Height and Roundness: She goes to the doorway and bends over to start at one bottom corner, tracing her fingertips on the arch of the plaster wall until she has reached the other bottom corner. She does not finish off the shape. That would be stupid, like circles, which are stupid and hateful. Triangles at least can be cracked at a corner. It is easy to reach up and around the doorway because she is tall and can reach up easily. She doesn't bend at the knees when she goes down, just lets her waist swing her down quickly, expertly.

4. Kissing and Slope: It is also easy to kiss him because he is tall. When his hands are attached to her hips she can look him straight into the eye. They are equivalent. This is why she doesn't mind him matching up his body with girls of various sizes. The numbers don't lie, she could always say, if she had to. There are parallels going from earth to heaven and his delta y is the same as her delta y. As for the slope, when they are standing up it is undefined, although she can picture it (straight up and down) and when they are lying down it is 0 (flat). So many lines have the same slope it is ridiculous. They may as well all be the same, walking around with the same damn slope all the fucking time. It doesn't matter. They all have the same slope. "You scumbag you maggot you cheap lousy faggot." She knows there must be more of that, or at least some little edge to bend down.

PRACTICE QUESTION
Define in some setting some other than urban financial rampage setting how boyfriend girlfriend line segment touching line segment only to form a non-slope that is defined.

ANS: It's not that she can't imagine herself in some other role. Some other incredibly buxom role, actually. If there were a bar/whorehouse combination somewhere in Wyoming, then she would be the madam/bartender combination that went along with. She would have much longer hair than any other bartender, and she would tie it up loosely so it was falling down around her riveting eyes. In general she would have a look that says, old-west-power-whore. The sheriff comes in, she slams down a drink and a lip curl with a snappy sex comment. There's trouble in the bar, rowdy boys wanting kisses from some shy bitch in yellow. Slap the bitch, slap the boys around with them laughing, her bending at the waist a lot, backwards, face keeping quiet calm no matter what she's saying. Looking around. Keeping an eye. Some bad gun slingers she would fuck herself. They would die for her lower lip. They would tattoo her name (starting with a J) onto their horses for luck.

9.3 CIGARETTES

When defining the terms of line and sentence and thing and especially when line and penis and sentence coincide on the labial plane, it is useful to apply a manual transitional aid. For the reduction of cigarettes there is fire and physics. For the reduction of penis there is cold water fat ugly whores and wrenching pulls that are too much to excite.

EX. In the car on the way to Buffalo from Detroit, she has refused to drive because they are not on the freeway anymore, nor are they in the city. They are on some shitass winding country road and half the time it is behind some lard carrying white truck. She has written these four torturous sentences onto some cigarettes and while she plays with them in her hand she wishes he would turn around and look at her doing it. He won't drive either. It might be erotic. Position one is when she is looking straight at the cigarette so she can read the sentence on the side. By rotating the cigarette away from her she can reach position two when the sentence is on top of the cigarette and to her is readable as a flat black line. There would be a similar effect if she wrote the sentence on a piece of paper, put the piece of paper on a table, and then looked at the sentence from table level. It would appear to be a flat black line. Position three is when she is looking at the end of the cigarette, so it appears to have no length, only width, and the sentence appears as a black mark on the circumference of it. Of course if the cigarette were a truly theoretical line, this manipulation would result in a point with no width, and the sentence would automatically be reduced. Curvature is getting in the way, as usual she pretends to ignore it, but it isn't fair. She realizes in the course of this study that there is a fourth position of infinite variety, where the cigarette is tilted away from her, neither perpendicular nor parallel in angle. It can appear to be anywhere from .01 to 5 inches long, or any length in between, depending on how she moves her fingers. Of course she can always move her head to accommodate, but why should she have to? It is a line. It has length. What makes it fucking do that. He asks her if she has a cigarette and she automatically hands him the one she is messing with. Good thing he trusts her not to give him a cigarette with ink on it and her hand sweat on it. She can lean back against the door and then bend her legs to rest her feet on the other door handle (annoying). He sucks carefully on the cigarette, blows a little smoke out and then sucks it back in, blows it out again and the car window stops it. She watches the burned part grow longer until she really wants him to ash it, watches the words disappear into the tiny black drawer under the radio, scattered. First it says "bag you maggot you cheap lousy faggot". Then it says "got you cheap lousy faggot", then "faggot" on the filter. Maybe his way is better.

9.4 Sex

The reason they do not have sex is easy. The shortest

distance between two points is a line. It's not that she cares, what the slope of the line is, or where she falls or he falls on it, but it's got to be one line. It's the shortest distance. The equation of a line is y=mx+b with m being the slope. With the heads pointing toward positive infinity on the x axis (one likes to be positive) the slope of the average female in missionary position is about 0.25 while the slope of the average male is 0.47 when m=(x2-x1)/(y2-y1). (See figure 9.4a) It can be seen that these are two different lines, not even taking into account the displacement from the x axis or bed. Merely the slope will show. So, for them to actually have intercourse, they would have to spread their legs and come together with their heads facing directly away, like two pairs of scissors trying to cut each other. (See figure 9.4b) This was hard on his dick, and hard on her to jostle up against him in that ungainly way. Maybe in space, in a vacuum, it could be accomplished, but on earth with its gravity, it was pretty much useless.

Figure 9.4a Slope and Sex, Missionary Position

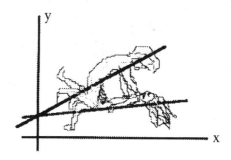

Figure 9.4b Slope and Sex, Linear Position

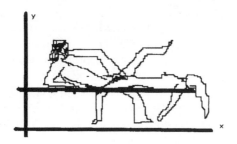

Practice Question:
Define then this other woman syndrome marking clearly
your work and showing the inaccurately otherly woman in
such a wifely way as to portray them as equivalent or then
in some way provide a rational graph to prove that they are
non-linear.

ANS: It's not that she can't imagine him in other roles.
She imagines him fully clothed, in a prison camp for men,
in some northern almost arctic region. He would have to
fight. He would have to use his mind and be clever to
survive, and it would be a daily struggle. The overbearing
slave driver or prison lord or overseer or captain would
identify with him and they can have a destructive interesting relationship. Sometimes the captain sets him up for a
fall, knowing he may be damaged. To the captain, her
boyfriend represents survival. The captain makes him do
the hardest work, taking on the sharpest knife machine in

the lumber yard, a machine which he is not really physically prepared to control. The boyfriend is aware of all this. He is tragically aware. Is he wrongfully imprisoned? He is definitely not imprisoned for any great national issue or political reason. He was probably arrested in a scuffle, with his dick in a whore. With him at the prison camp he has a picture of a woman. If he is in the top bunk then he keeps it under his pillow. If he is in the bottom bunk, he puts it above him, between the mattress of the top bunk man and the metal mesh that makes square lines across the picture. The woman is his soulmate, he loves her mind. He loves her. They are so compatible it is like they are meant to be together. And the beauty of it is, he isn't even sure if she has a pussy or not, because he has never pressed the issue. Possibly he imagines that between her legs it is smooth and soft, unhairy, confusingly sweet-smelling. Her boyfriend has this beautiful picture and it is of her.

Questions For Review:
1. Using the techiques of Jenny Larson Phantasm Sexpot Genius, reduce the sentences of which we speak to linear constructs, and if the narrative should follow then at least regroup and multiply. Find at least five ways to operate this reduction, graphing answers when convenient. Do not resolve a logical proof of the sentences. In light of the Buffalo trip, this has become unnecessary.

Ans.
    a.) If the sentences had been bodies, she would have torn the limbs off and arranged them easily: arm, arm, torso, leg, leg, arm, arm, torso, leg, leg, arm, arm, torso, leg, leg,

arm, arm, torso, leg, leg. Then there would be a repeating pattern. Or she could have done it arm arm torso leg leg leg leg torso arm arm arm arm torso leg leg leg leg torso arm arm, so there was a connection between the different people's limbs, like touching like.

b.) If they had been one continuous sentence, or even a logical paragraph, then there would be s's to unravel and connect to straightened out c's. There would be rules to follow, like the cross on a t or f gets lined up after the letter it crosses, not before. Letters get toppled to the right not the left so the bottom part of the l goes to the left of the top part. She tries writing them out in cursive, trying each combination and working out if there is any logical progression to be found. There are 24 such combinations and none of them are logical. If the cursive curly ends of the words could be pasted together, and the periods between sentences could become part of the continuous line, then if the very ends were pulled sharply the entire thing would snap out straight, and the crosses and loops would sort themselves out through the sheer force of the snap. They might go flying off into space, or they might get twisted in and join the rest of the line. It just depends on how hard the snap is.

she chose the wrong city

c.) Perhaps she could stack the sentences on top of each other and with compression force them down onto the bottom one until they were mashed into a line. This would result in a line four times too thick, at least. Width, curvature, almost a tube.

you scumbag you maggot you cheap lousy faggot
there is a reason he hasn't been around in a week
she chose the wrong city to live in and died there
i am the superbeing you have never yet detected

d.) Write the sentences down in cursive and then outlining each word in dark ink. These outlines can then be traced onto tracing paper and arranged, like with like, until a pattern is reached and some linear progression becomes obvious.

e.) Make a list of all the words independently and then arrange them all on a graph, which is a method suggested by a friend, with various schemes in mind — location geographically, relative importance to the sentence, proximity to meaninglessness (the word "to" being close to absolute zero, the word "she" being far from it, the word "faggot" placed far from zero but in the negative direction). These points could then be connected in the shape of a duck or a flower, or something, and then this final line could be stretched out to a satisfying straightness.

CHAPTER REVIEW:

In Buffalo, they are unable to locate the Buffalo Tap because the friend is along. At the Buffalo Tap, they would have been sitting correctly, at the bar, with her in the middle and the men on either side, she could turn from one to the other by rotating her head 180 degrees. The friend could be talked to when the boyfriend was being evasive, and the boyfriend could be talked to when the friend started referencing composers she didn't know. But the very threat of the friend makes the Buffalo Tap inaccessible, and they settle at a coffee place with thick wood tables where the waitress clears the ashtray every time they take a drag. They are in a triangle and everyone is trying to think in two directions. Friend: influence boyfriend on life decisions, maintain clever knowing commentary with girlfriend. Girlfriend: keep friend talking about unrelated subjects, connect with boyfriend in some way to show she is smart and on top of things. Boyfriend: make friend think he is being influential on life decisions, get girlfriend's sincere reactions to life decision regarding the proposed Buffalo move. The dynamic is just fucked. Yet they stay there interminably. She could announce that they will never get it going and that she cannot operate under these fucked conditions. She could make trips to the bathroom to avoid feeling claustrophobic. It is also too hot in the coffee place and the windows are starting to get steamed up. She hates being there.

Theorem of Boyfriend Rectal Blowtorch Activity:

"Look," he says, "This math stuff you do is just your extraneous bullshit. But it's interesting, don't get me wrong."

CHAPTER TEST:

In essay form accomplish three goals. 1.) Get out of this mess about lines and sentences. 2.) Invent a vaginal device to make the penis slide easily into the fourth dimension or if possible into another universe altogether. 3.) Create a concept which resolves the girl/boy/girl problem of linearity and slope. You have 50 minutes. It is not necessary to show your work any more.

Playing with paper. She has this paper. Cutting it with a scissors into a long strip she wraps it around her arm, around her waist, around her neck, then flattens it out on the table in front of her. There. Looks at it suspiciously. Then she bends it around into a circle, the flatness creating a dumb, bad, blunt edge. Circles remind her of people's heads. Holding the circle up with one finger dangling it off she puts her fist through it sharply several times. She takes the ends of the strip away from each other, puts a twist in it, and puts them back together what a science project would define as moebius. Seeing this, she gets tape, she gets a marker, and writes onto this one-sided whirl the sentences in a row which come around to meet each other and do not have a back and cannot be unspun. She will be careful not to put her fist through this one. It might disappear, or become anti-dimensional this is a line one dimension this is not to be put through. If she can put it into her vagina, it will wreak havoc with his penis, she is sure.

She puts her eyes closed and they are both as points on the road to infinity, along this axis or that, probably parallel to the x axis but crossing the y axis at -2, perpetually negative though headed in the positive direction. They will be moving at varying speeds that do not interfere with each other, because constantly separated by a delta x of 2(years). Perhaps at some point they will cross the x axis and join the first quadrant, become positive. This with the advent of possible children. He would be tender. Making their equation into $y=(.02)x-2$, and $x=x1+.5$, $x=x1+1$, $x=x1+1.5$, and on, where x1 seems currently to be November 28, 1994.

Upstairs Alan in the Room

I'll get him, I'll take it up to him, I'll take it up, when he wakes up I'll take it up to him, I'll make it first, before he wakes up and then I'll take it up to him, before he wakes up, I'll make it, you stay asleep. Great.

I'm not coming down today, he says, *You're family isn't what I thought they would be, especially when your sister is so smart.*

Is Alan coming down today? No.
Is he coming down to breakfast this morning?
NO. I'll take it up to him. I cooked it already.
How early did you get up anyway?
Four o'clock this morning.
Dad was up at four, and gone.
(Dad, you always get up this early?
I'm leaving for Alabama. Alabama?)
Alan isn't coming down.
He didn't come down at all, did he?
I know.

Upstairs Jane's old room takes up the back of the house. In one corner is Dad's desk which is an antique and thousands of little papers are shoved into the pigeonholes all notes from sermons or returned checks or receipts. The chair can roll around on the cheap linoleum floor and can recline. Then a sewing machine, the kind that folds down into the stand and has a foot pedal to run it, with more little drawers in the stand, buttons, thread. What she loves, the thing she used to put into her mind — Dad had this one ram when they had the sheep farm here, of all the sheep, the ram was biggest, and when it died he had the head mounted. It was Dad's ram so she asked where are you going to put the head, and he didn't want to look at it all the time. It hurt him to know the ram was dead, because it had been such a bad, recalcitrant ram. So he put it in her room over her bed, with its glass eyes. Those brown fake eyes could move and follow you, but not be mean to her, just to whatever might come in there — by this time she was in high school and really too old to care about the dark. Now Alan makes a lump in the bed under light green ribbed covers. He speaks to her when she comes in.

Look, I think your family is like, I mean where did your sister come from? Not from them. Where is she from? What, what are you looking at?

Dad is leaving right now for Alabama.

Bye, Dad. He laughs and says bye again. To the wall. And waves his hand kind of weakly. Very weakly. Janie picks his hand up off the bed where it fell.

No more aspirin today she says perkily.

Why don't you go to fucking hell?

No more aspirin she says under her breath real low — some religious fanatic he is.

Your father is going all the way to Alabama for what — to preach in some pissant church for five dollars? Some church? Look, he preaches in some church in Alabama and people can't put more than a penny in the collection plate, but they're all quiet then. They're quiet for that whole time, for an hour while he preaches to them and then putting in the penny, all they can put into the collection plate. It's sick. Anyone who wasn't stupid would see that.

So she says, standing in the doorway of the room with the doorknob in her hand, while she twists the doorknob around in her hand. The dress she is wearing is orange and a little extreme, length-wise. Her father thought, or said, that it was a little extreme, but said it so funny that it was obvious he didn't care and was happy she had nice dresses. Did Alan buy the dress for her? Did Alan have that kind of money? Alan bought her a book another book five more books and she let him borrow them right back immediately because they would help him with Bible study and all the writing he was doing. The books he read made his eyes bad. The aspirin he took for the arthritis he had made his stomach bad, bad. He was sick today and not coming down. Again.

Good, she says *so did you want the coffee or the tea?* She didn't really want to get involved in talking back to the things he said because as soon as that happened it was like asking him to make her feel like an idiot and why should she go through that on her vacation? A long weekend from school.

Or whatever.

Alan is small under the covers, and his thick hair hangs in his eyes and makes him look sullen. His toes are shifting his feet back and forth rhythmically at the foot of the bed. He's got a book there by his hand, his hand is keeping it open with one finger, keeping the page open. She is looking at that ram's head and thinking about how she used to do it. In the pasture she, gymnast, would jump up on the ram and over him and he was not quick enough, and when he got raving and dangerous chasing her, she vaulted high over the fence and out. The ram sitting there mad at the barbed wire, hungry, mad. She was bad to that ram.

Her sister, Ramona, has a very high IQ.

Janie stands in the doorway and waits for the coffee/tea answer, but he probably won't give it to her, so she goes back to the stairs and waits a little longer, then she sits down right on the stairs. Now the room is Ramona's room really, she took it over for no reason. Janie sits upstairs on the top step with the breakfast tray in her hand and he has taken the toast and a little of the juice and then set all the plates right back on the tray, hasn't eaten the eggs (never eats eggs).

This little man? her small harsh mother had said. *This little man is Alan? What happened to Tim Stover, at least he had a little height to him.*

Janie stands up and goes downstairs with the tray.

I'm going up there, says Ramona, taking one look at the tray back in the kitchen *and tell him where he's gone wrong.*

No, says Janie, *leave him alone can't you?*

The little weasel, says the sister, Ramona, the smartie.

Shut up, shut the fuck up, thinks Jane. She never even swears out loud to Alan. And Alan can fucking swear.

I'm going says Ramona.

Mother, Jane throws the tray into the sink never mind if it breaks and cuts and kills everyone. Never mind if everyone who puts their dumb hands into that sink forever and ever gets a big piece of glass in between their fingers and it keeps on cutting in and festering and messing with their bloodstream and maybe going up into their hearts and then becoming lodged in the smaller blood vessels of the brain and killing their dumb stupid asses.

Don't throw dishes, says the sister, as if it is a habitual thing, and the mother goes over there with a piece of bread and mops up the glass. *Stay away from him* says the mother to the sister without looking at Jane, as if Jane is in no way connected to the him they are discussing. *I knew him at school before she knew him,* says Ramona, *We used to have lunch together. I knew him first. I thought he was an idiot.*

You thought he was an asshole. There's a difference, says Jane with tremendous spunk and knowing it is kind of shocking but not really because she has heard Dad say Ass before, dear funny fix-it Dad who has safety pins holding his car together and a bad looking blue shirt for his Sunday best under kind of a crappy suit.

Super-Ramona, thinner, prettier, smarter, can't flirt because she's shy and no boy has ever touched her, she's so weird that no boy even could touch her, they couldn't get that close. The sisters used to sleep in the same room in the same bed and they used to fight about if there were squirrels in the closet or if there were dead things in there.

Dad is back. His car broke and he walked back and it's already noon and so he must have had to walk pretty far why didn't he just call? He didn't call because. He's cold and tickles his girls.

Daddy, look, I'm going up to that boy and drag him down here where we can talk to him, says Ramona crabbily.

Why do you want to talk to him, says Dad.

He still won't come out of his room. How rude, Ramona stares at the floor.

Look says Jane as a distraction, *I'll tell you a funny story about college in Wheaton Illinois at my school. About college, let me see, okay.*

There was this girl, real pretty girl. She started dating this super rich guy, and one time got asked over to his house for dinner, and it was huge, the house was enormous. When she had to go to the bathroom she said quietly to his mother, Where is the POWDER ROOM, to be cool and not to sound crude, because you can't say where's the john in a house like that. [the father and mother and sister are all in the kitchen and now Jane has her back to the sink where the remains of this tray is mushed together, the eggs, the jam, the juice, some of it has glass in it] *But this girl found out that the POWDER ROOM was just that, no toilet, and she didn't want to sound like an idiot and go back downstairs saying no I meant the toilet, so she just thought okay I'll pee in the sink. Okay, so while she was sitting in the sink and peeing, it FELL OFF THE WALL and she hit her head somehow and passed out and woke up and there was this guy and his family sitting around asking each other what could she have been doing, in a puddle of pee with her pants around her ankles and the sink ripped out of the wall.*

The sister Ramona is laughing very hard, thinks it's very funny. The father is trying to laugh without looking at the mother, who doesn't think it was funny at least she is not letting on.

There, thinks Jane, Janie, good funny girl.

She goes back upstairs and he doesn't look at her for two hours, just reads his book very fast turning the pages rapidly and never stopping to ask her if she understood that part when she read the book, or if she read the book, he coughs as if he has crap in his throat.

She thinks about sinus medication, allergy medication.

She thinks about spending money on pills, spending on pills, pills.

He has allergies to dust three, mold three and four, she had looked at the list that was sitting out, he had been looking at it. Try to figure out why his allergies get worse or better. She can't think about it when people are downstairs waiting.

Cheerful, cheerful, cheerful. Later, Daddy is calling to get some parts for the car, then to walk back out there and fix it *on the fly* he says like it's still driving while he's fixing it. Funny daddy, funny good girl Janie, good Janie, making a man come home with her at last to see them, that man, the Alan one that Ramona talks about, Ramona who did better at that school, the same school as them all.

Ramona is in the kitchen ripping up newspapers because it makes them lighter to carry out to the trash place and they burn better. When Jane passes through on her way to the bathroom (the downstairs is circular, like old houses often are) Ramona raises her voice trying to figure out a way that Daddy won't have to walk all the way out there, because Mother has a car but it's also broken right at the moment, up on some crates in the executive parking lot as they call the gravel part by the house. *Alan has a car,* she says, *why can't he give Dad a ride out to his car?*

You know he's sick, says Jane acidly from the bathroom peeing.

He's not sick.

Jane lets all the water fill back into the toilet and the tank before she opens the door and comes out. Ramona is waiting for a couple more days and then going back out to Rhode Island where she lives with her college roommate and the roommate's husband and their foster kids. She teaches in this experimental school for young children, she's a really good teacher, young, fresh out of college. But they're on break right now and her Dad brought her home in his car, it was on his way home from a week of meetings in New England.

I'll drive his car, says Jane, *I'll go get the keys from him.*

Ramona says, *I'll drive his stupid car.*

When she gets into the room his eyes are closed but she can't tell if she's asleep. She strokes his forehead with her fingertips and he moans with satisfaction. Maybe he is really sick. She looks around for his jacket, his khaki military looking jacket with the very warm lining.

What are you looking for Jane he says and she jumps and says *the keys.*

You're not driving the car, and I'm not well enough, so why do you want the keys? What could you possibly want the keys for?

Dad's car is broken down all the way to Emlenton, practically, and so I was going to drive him out there with the parts to fix it, if you don't mind.

No.

She stands there smiling a little residual smile and

getting mad. He doesn't open his eyes, but he pulls her hand back toward his face, to continue touching him, as if she doesn't feel mad at all. Then Janie feels sad. Actually, what if she broke the car. It is a manual transmission and her car in Wheaton is automatic. Why had they taken his car to get here, when they could have taken hers? Why had they taken a road trip to Pennsylvania when they could have stayed in Illinois. Why had she wanted him to meet them, when she knew he would just get overtired from the trip?

I'm sorry, she says. *Really.*

He smiles a little soft smile that might mean he's sorry too. That he can't get out of bed.

Ramona doesn't see it like that. *That's it,* she says when she finds out, when Janie tells them in a hushed voice, *I'm the only one who's sick of it I guess,* so she stomps her feet all the way upstairs like a frustrated child trying to make a point.

You are the most repulsive piece of dog doo. Ramona often uses language like this. *You are the most ridiculous mess of a human being. I hate you. I hate your life. My father is too nice to hate you so I have to hate you instead. You think my stupid sister knows anything? You think she knows what you are? You are dog doo. That's what you are.* She is mad beyond keeping her voice down below where her father can hear. She is so mad it makes the room feel exciting. His eyes are half closed as if he is dreaming, as if he likes it and it makes him feel good. Janie stands in the hall crying because Ramona called her stupid and because everything had turned out awful. Why couldn't they have brought her car? Why did she have to be so stupid?

Blanket Stealers and the Women Who Love Them

Cross referencing under the categories "home drama" and "belligerence," we find "sleep patterns" and "conflict" cohabitating. Under "women" we find "my problem and how I solved it" mourning its sibling "I'm not even going to worry about something that stupid" which is filed irrevocably under "men."

Case Study:

In the morning he is only too happy to give them all back. She is a forgiving sort, saying that anything was permissible, even cheating (on a moment by moment basis) but over time even breathing could be grounds for divorce. Or blanket stealing. Our standard of life is very high, he would say, if you think about it. You live in a house you eat food your life is quiet and sweet do you know what the people in London for example have to contend with? You deserve a hardship. You have a bed and clothes that don't stink of piss. What do you want, the world? She forgave him intolerance, lack of insight, pettiness, greed, insatiability, irrationality, and disdain on a daily basis. But she has a safety net — which you can all try at home. And that is. Each time forgive a very large *percent* of the crime. Leave a remnant. Like cleaning out a house that gets continually flooded with new rocks. Every time the rocks come, you clear away most of them, you make a real effort at cleaning, but you leave just a few rocks each time. Eventually the house is full of rocks and then you move out. So with blanket stealing for Booney and Cluck.

You tried to kill me last night she screamed. *Look at me!*

Don't you know that most myths aren't true? But some are.
Here are some examples. You can quiz yourself.

Myth #1: Men become different people at night when they are asleep. They steal blankets out of a base animal desire to survive through the cold winter night. True or False? False. If they were awake and really really cold they would do the same thing, only they would pretend to be asleep. Now you can't pretend to be dominated by your base animal will. If you pretend — that's trickery. So sleep is just pretending that has gotten comfortable and gone real. A subterfuge. A means to sneak without having to go through the motions because you are doing the motions because you are really asleep. The ultimate fake is something actually real. And then he can steal them. STEALER!

Myth #2: The blanket is a form of birth control. The woman robbed of her blanket feels susceptible to invasion by genetic material. True or false? True. Obviously. Even the most rugged mountain sperm cannot set off across a blanket with any accuracy or hope of survival. Peeling a blanket off a sleeping woman is like peeling a diaphragm off a cervical gap. Here is the key. It's different when you're awake. When you're awake a blanket can be a prop, an accessory to coyness, a lovely little hiding thingy, a way to creep around the house naked — a blanket can be a gown or a tent or a plaything but it's different when you're asleep and you don't know what's going on — just suddenly awake and cold and him wrapped firmly up in all the blankets — have to practically skin him to get in there where he is.

Myth #3: A woman with a really good body image doesn't need a blanket because if she were any sort of a woman she'd be naked and free assuming of course the heat is on. True or false? False. The important element is chin blanket contact. This has nothing to do with body content or long tall short anything. Here's the pivotal sequence: weight on right side, right arm tucked under head, reach around with the left arm, grab the blanket and pull it up to the chin covering the shoulder. Repeat if you want this gorgeous exercise without a blanket and find your empty fist striking your chin so ragefully that you will blame him forever.

While driving through Wisconsin they judge the small towns by the number of little round emblems the townspeople have hung on their population sign. For example: Rotary Club, Keep Greenwood Clean Committee, National State District Baseball Champions. *But Loyal had six of them honey,* he says incredulously. *Loyal is a fucking small ass town.* In Loyal she lifts her arms above her head for him to take her shirt off lovingly before a bath. And she has two bruised arms. He is alarmed. He suspects her of hitting and inflicting herself which is something so monstrous. *You better think of a good reason for this if you intend to wear your brown dress to work,* he says. *No one's going to believe you smacked your head on the dryer.* They drive through the Midwest because they love the accents. They cannot believe how people don't realize they have accents. They are amazed by simply everything. They like seeing the signs like "Innovative House of Music. Pellia Pellet, Instructor" which is spelled out in relentless block print. They revel in the fact that they could live anywhere, that they are young and have no friends.

Here are some questions to ask yourself if you are having blanket problems:

Do I really need a blanket?
Wouldn't I be much better off with just no blanket?
If I had no blanket, what other thing could I occupy my mind with to stop myself from whining?
If I must whine, how can I stuff a potato down my throat

to stop myself from being audible?
If he hears me whining, how can I explain that I was just checking the radiators and they are just fine?
If he fails to believe my lie, how can I find a piano wire in this apartment?
If I fail to find a piano wire, how can I find something just as sharp?

She wakes up in a vise grip hearing him muttering something disenchanted. *Nothing you mutter has any conviction,* she thinks. She turns her face to his and breathes in his nasty cigarette breath dutifully. She likes him to stop muttering. *Look at us sleeping here together like two lovers* she thinks. *Rachel* he mutters. She thinks *Dear god, even him.* What if she gets bruises from claustrophobia? What if she gets bruises from sheer love? What if they come right out of her arm like a hopeful explosion of passionate emotion? He tightens his grip on her throat and she knows that fifty times tomorrow she will not be able to take in a full breath, even if she waits for it, even if she yawns, she will not be able to fill her lungs up all the way. But now at this moment it's not based on stress or imagination. Now it's based on strangulation. When he rolls over he takes the blankets with him.

Case Study:

For Booney, it's about grace. She doesn't go dangling all over the bed with her legs here and her feet way down there all straggling over the edge. It's about unity. For Cluck it is a question of — What's the matter I've got leprosy or something? wanting her to stay wrapped arms and legs around him unmovable even in death or sleep (which is death but impermanent). Problem is that Cluck falls asleep immediately and immediately moves into combat zone — meaning this for me that for you and *that* is nothing but breeze and a little corner of bed that's been menstruated on. *It's as though you want to win or something* says she tempestuously over the morning tea. *It's like you can't really rest until I'm completely miserable. Whoa* says he laughing *I am asleep here god damn it. How can I have this capacity? You fall asleep too soon I have to get away from you when you're asleep* says she *you're violent and you moan things out and you thrash and whip them off me you put your hand under next to my skin slowly down and then whip real quick off they come you are calculating it's awful.*

She will build him a cage and never reveal it to anyone. She will protect him from the potential stigma of wife-beater, woman-eater. From his sleep he pulls things like burned paintings, disappointment in the academy, divorce, death. How can he not upon waking pummel her into a wound? How can he be restrained? She would never no not for one second contend that his helpless violence was not intentional. Not to deny credit, when credit is so valuable, coming at a price of a thousand dollars at least. It's simply a desire not to receive the whaling. It implies no judgment. Who is she to judge. Perhaps so brave as to flaunt it in front of people, her short sleeves. Perhaps so cheerful on going down for a nap as to curl in pleasure and say I am so happy. Stretching over the entire bed when he uses the bathroom. Thinking him in his cage and me under every blanket that has ever been lovingly sewn. And really, metaphysically, quite close. When two people are bound by a unifying principle, can even sex unite them more effectively? No-body really wants to hit nice little people like her.

Here are some quick tips for women who love blanket stealing men.

#1. You will have fewer problems with blanket stealing if you are on the downhill side of the bed. Blankets are, like so many things, affected by gravity. Therefore they tend to "gravitate" toward the lowest side of the bed. Even if you don't think your bedroom floor is sloping, I bet it is. Even if you have measured it and measured it and laid a level on the floor and it was right smack in the middle I bet you have missed some little thing. I bet if you did it just one more time you would notice the slight incline on your side of the bed. Or you could do another thing. You could gain some weight, and with the soft-ness of your mattress your valley that you create with your body would surpass his valley and through gravity the blankets and him and everything will come sliding gladly into your valley. Use gravity to keep your blankets. Gravity is an unknown ally in this matter.

#2. Smack him with an open handed smack. *This* will rouse him.

#3. One of our readers wrote in this clever trick. She calls it "ordering up recruits" but you might like to call it "having a teammate." She puts an extra blanket at the foot of the bed and then at 3:00 am when she is having the dream about little house on the prairie the early years, she can wake up, pull that blanket over her, and have it all to herself. There is in fact nothing more satisfying than having all your blankets removed and then having just that one extra. Here's the secret to the success of this little trick: A man will only steal blankets once a night. Once he has got them all, safely tucked around his buttocks and slung between his clamped triumphant legs, he will not return to the hunting ground to bring down a second quarry.

I hope you didn't buy this magazine just to look at this sex article, he says in the you're naughty you smart beautiful child voice. *No, I bought it to look at the pictures of bodies I'll never have. And the horoscopes.* He putters around, picking up things and putting them down in better places. He can raise his hands, swing them around, reach up high, she can see the muscles in his neck. It inspires in her no deep subsurface cringe. *You used to like it when I read women's magazines* she screams at him from her chair that she has picked apart neurotically, beyond recognition, without thinking about it once. *I'm afraid to turn my back on you. I used to love sleeping pills and now I hate them and now I wouldn't take one if you begged me on your knees.*

Interview:

Cluck: LOOK I CANNOT HELP IT I AM ASLEEP!
Booney: Well I don't know why you have to be so mean.
LJ: So, where did you guys meet?
Booney: He used to be perfect.
LJ: Like, in a nightclub or something?
Booney: He still is sort of.
LJ: So, when did this problem start?
Booney: He used to strap his hands together behind his back and sleep on his face. It's when the unstrapping happened that the troubles began.
LJ: Unstrapping?
Booney: Yes, unconsciously, even in "sleep" if you believe in it, he can unstrap himself and get free.
LJ: You make him wear handcuffs to bed? To sleep?
Booney: Oh yes. Sure.
Cluck: LOOK I CANNOT HELP IT I AM ASLEEP!
Booney: You'll never know the constant constant horror, because if you turn the heat up, you just roast.
Cluck: I. AM. ASLEEP.
Booney: Because that's the night he decides to be human.
LJ: Booney, don't you think he might just be asleep?
Booney: He's never just asleep.
Cluck: IT'S A BLANKET!

Very old television programs have proven that it is possible for married people to sleep in separate beds.

The Pretty Lunatic Theory

The last of the world's great unchained beasts lies at the foot of my bed she thinks. His name is Doggydog she thinks. How unlikely this is, yet true. She sits up in bed and motions for Doggydog to wake. *Now you pretend that I am hard to read and you can't trust me,* says she to Doggydog. *Just for a minute, and then we'll switch back to where you say I am a cold unfeeling animal and I have no heart.* (typical) The story begins in Muffy's bed when Doggydog wakes up and smiles at her with his snaggletooth mouth. *Doggydog is a mean bad mans* she says, tugging at his ears and rubbing the top of his head. *I'm not pretending anything you stupid bitch* he says stretching out his legs. He is cramped in his space. She forgets to feed him about every third day. His dick is interesting.

Look I have a tight schedule today. I have to go to the post office and also I have to go look for an apartment with Ramona and Dave. When she says this, if successful, there is a great purpose in her words. *I'm just going to hang out and drink beer and listen to tunes* says Doggydog, *then later you can take me out to eat.* Sighing over Doggydog, she picks up his morning shit off the floor and strokes it lovingly (holy shit). *Nice shit* she thinks, *so round and beautiful.* His clothes spread everywhere on the furniture and no matter how many times she scrubs them they retain the odor of rot. There are clumps of fur sticking out of the cuffs and neckholes as if his shedding were widespread, yet he manages to shed on everything all the time never losing enough hair to actually be bald although patchy. Doggydog is practically a full time job in himself. He needs to be taken for walks, to the bookstore, out for Korean, to the nervous vet in the heart of the city. Doggydog is still sucking on his morning cigarette after she has showered (purposefully), made coffee (for him), and gotten dressed (in private).

LETTER TO DAD
part one... age 16

Dear Dad

Don't you want to be my daddy? Don't you want me as your sweet baby darling? Look at my accomplishments. Look at my successes. See I array them in attractive formations around your doorstep and gaze up at you lovingly fingering one then the other and saying with my dear precious eyes I LOVE YOU. I am an oddity. A superkid. I have done all my work, I have shown all my steps, I have retrieved every ball ever thrown and not with haste or malice but with care dear loving care. See me. I am a cute little button. I am a joyful little puppy (wag). SEE ME SEE ME.
Love, Muffy

Interview with Alan Friere:

LJ: So...
AF: Well, I consider myself really to be Muffy's pride
and joy. What could be more romantically necessary than
the villainous and absent father? That's why she has
all her friends. That's why she is viable as a lunatic.
You know you can't be cleverly insane without the
benefit of a terrible family circumstance. And her
mother was really nice. I'm basically the motivating
factor behind everything she's ever done that's
interesting or notable. So. How bad do you feel now,
Ms. Accuser?

Outside the day is clear and beautiful. Ramona her sister
is waiting at the corner on her bicycle. *Muffy get rid of those
dorks* she says firmly. Muffy turns to see the straggling hord
of dorks rambling after her scrapping with each other,
fussing with their pants, adjusting their odors, and staring
pleasantly around. She counts them off by days of the week,
and they disperse, making notes in their daybooks. *When
they are around me their lives are interesting* says Muffy. *Think
again* says Ramona, *a girl who wants what she can never have
gives off a certain scent.* Muffy's hair is beautifully colored
each hair red gold brown and it is long so that it could easily
cover her whole body. She keeps it tied up in a rope while
it is still wet from the shower, and this trick gives it a
fascinating twist. She and Ramona tramp through the city
with grand noises and high minded conversation. They are
girls but Ramona is twenty years older and has met Muffy's

father. There is all this horridly complicated family stuff going on. Unnecessary, impractical, deliberately torturous enough to be left out.

They need to hurry to get to the apartment they are going to look at. They rush and tap tap on the pavement. Ramona's wrinkles drop and rise a little bit with each tap to prove they have achieved or maintained some degree of sproingyness. Muffy can explain as they go how the different neighborhoods denote different levels of stability. She can paint on the sidewalk sketches of men she would have to marry to live in these houses. For this neighborhood she draws rampantly uncut hair and skinny and unwashed. Something like Doggydog. There are scummy things in the gutters here and the girls don't brush their hair and the men don't walk very fast. She has lived here at some point, or else she has dated someone here, or she has walked through, or she has heard about it, or she was born here. *You weren't born here*, says Ramona unkindly. She catches all Muffy's lies.

The next neighborhood curves around little red cobblestone streets appearing very old and ancient yet smelling sweet like lilacs. This is the ultimate wealth. The houses meld into the street fluidly and creak in the joints with age and legitimacy. Nothing rises over two storeys, as if proximity to the ground were an earned right. There are certainly a lot of windows facing the street. People have to have views. People cannot be forced to stare at brick walls and fire escapes. People have rights and privileges. While she is sketching out the man Ramona notices a car in the driveway of one of these houses. *Look it is a Bumper and a vintage Bumper. Now I wonder. Which would be better*. Muffy stares at the bright black car which is low to the ground and definitely sedate but curvy. *Would it be better to have owned this car in the year it was made and kept hold of it, or would it be better to have decided to purchase this car lately and to have had a bank account capable of handling the purchase price?* Muffy and Ramona stand next to the car as if posing for a snooty magazine. They pretend to be talking about something fabulous as they argue this point. Holding hands sometimes and sometimes kissykissing on the movie star style cheeks they deliver their lines with brilliance and grace. *The time the time* says Muffy and they move on, walking quickly to avoid the newly converging swarm of dorky men who would like to ask someone special out on a date.

LETTER TO DAD
part two... the college years

Mailing address: Alan Friere
                      398 La Santa Blvd.
                      Apartment A
                      Los Angeles, CA

Method: Open box. Dump in shit from the files. Slap on mailing address from the phone book. Open another box. Dump in shit from files. Slap on mailing address from the phone book. Open box. Dump in shit from files. Slap on dad's address from grandma's letter. Open box. Dump in shit from files. Slap on mailing address from the phone book.

Contents: Newspaper clippings. letter from old boyfriends,

early poetry, class notes, flyers, announcements, cards, invitations, secret diaries, pages torn out of books, pictures, a smashed dried out table grape, discarded hats, empty shampoo bottles, little tiny plastic horses, post-its, reminders, printed out copies, and business cards.

NO cigarette butts (I don't smoke and I don't do BAD DRUGS)

Interview-with Muffy Franklin:

LJ: What are you doing there?

MF: I'm mailing out my possessions to strangers.

LJ: And what's the point of this little exercise?

MF: Well I've always thought it would be really neat to get something like this in the mail, you know, right off somebody's shelf. All this unsorted crap. Then you could make up little stories, or you could just be puzzled and think hmm wrong address but not me, I would never do that. I would most likely strike up a lifelong friendship, were I mailed something like this. I would make something timeless of it. Once I got a letter addressed to someone else. It was from this married woman, French by her grammar, and she was begging forgiveness to this prickish bastard, is my guess, who was saying that he couldn't meet her friends and he was all pissy about it. What does he need to meet her friends for? They have this beautiful love! She's married! Can you believe that? The luck? I mean, it wasn't exactly addressed to me or anything. I'll tell you this because I know you don't know any of the people in this city, but, it might explain my thing. It wasn't addressed to me and it was just laying on top of the

buzzers downstairs there. I kind of just took it. I'm
sorry.

She said to Doggydog once that she had no hope of ever
regulating her bowel. Even if I wake up and have a normal
shit, she said, I know that as soon as I get some cigarettes and
coffee in me, I'll have another shit which is diarrhea. I think
this is terrible. I am terrified of my own bowel. That's normal
said Doggydog. Everything you do is normal normal normal. It's absolutely normal to have diarrhea every day?
What if I have diarrhea eight times in a day? Is that okay?
Yes. Eight times a day. Normal, normal, normal. Asshole.

Interview with Doggydog:
MF: What are you some kind of loser barnacle?
DD: <squint, crouch, smoke, cross legs> The trouble
with Muffy, not that she's troubled, it's just a
trouble, is that she doesn't know how to hang out. She's
always saying to me. What are we doing tonight. You
know, we'll do what we do. It's like trying to impose
some sort of... I don't know limitude, like you can't
create something by making yourself create it. It just
happens. Like if Roland Barthe got up, scratched his
balls, and said I'm going to make up some theory. It
just doesn't happen in this manner. Now, please
understand, I accept, but I appreciate, I understand,
I encourage her desire to make money. I don't believe

in money myself. I'm an atheist.

Muffy was working on her drawing of the type of man she would have to marry to live in the apartment that Ramona wanted. She was involving several sidewalk squares in the effort, using the crack between them to mark his belt. I don't have to get married to live in this apartment said Ramona. I will never have to get married never my whole life and you see I am already fifty and I will have an apartment all on my own. Yet every week they went looking for one. Ramona should lower her sights. Ramona should stop trying to get placed into a married apartment. Muffy slaved over her drawing, trying not to make it into Dave as he moved down the street toward them. The thing was, it was actually Dave. The more she tried to squanch out the hips and make it a bulbous intellectual, the more it became a lanky and athletic supermodel. True, the apartment was modern. It had a ballroom.

Ramona chatted with the landlady using her most annoying full-tooth grin, to mean I am smarter and you are my tool, my TOOL. Muffy's hands were covered in sidewalk chalk dust, and turning up to Dave she said *I painted a picture of you, just for you, all for you. I invited you for the purpose of viewing this wonderful painting which I painted just for you.*

It doesn't look like me, he said, gazing at the camera, *It looks like another person. Some... Other... Person.*

Muffy grated her hands over the pavement in honor of erasing the blot to Dave's record. *No one will ever see it,* Dave, she promised. *No one no one.*

Come on you two, said Ramona. *Mrs. Plussize here wants*

to show the apartment now. She rolled her eyes as if Mrs. Plussize had chosen a strange time and a strange method for renting her real estate. Ramona paraded into the house, doing what she called a sashay, glancing to the right and to the left apparently noticing the niceties of It All. *Now here,* said Mrs. Plussize, *the application process begins.* In the lobby, outside the ballroom, stood a set of closet organizer bins all filled with colored sweaters. Each bin had a little mini-bin hooked to the front of it, and a metal bucket of colored eggs was on the floor. Muffy noticed that each mini-bin was suspiciously egg-shaped.

Now here, said Mrs. Plussize, *we find the absolute meaning of apartment searching. All the colors have to match.* She raised a stopwatch and glanced around the room ceremoniously. *GO!* she hollered, and Ramona quickly and with noticeable ease matched all the colored eggs with the sweaters of the same color. *Of course,* said Mrs. Plussize, *we could have found something more meaningful and symbolic than sweaters. But they are MY sweaters. That counts for something. And we all know nothing would be more symbolic than the immortal egg.*

While Muffy and Dave nodded seriously and forgivingly, Muffy's hand crept indelicately across the wall toward Dave's pantleg. She glanced at her hand and tried to will it back, tried to force it complacently to her side, but it WOULD go, and it tugged desperately at the neatly creased leg. It was a yearning little hand. Dave turned and swatted it away, firmly glaring at her upturned face and its vacuous grin of pure love. You have to really like people, she had read in a book, in order for them to like you. It has to be sincere. People can tell if you really like them, or if you are just gritting your teeth. She tried sincerely liking Dave for a full three minutes as Mrs. Plussize mumbled about times and standards and whether Ramona would make a good tenant, based on her score. She thought she could mark a significant warmth in Dave's response to her really honest affection. If necessary, she would drink Iced Tea for him. She knew he would never refer to it, as Dogboy did, as Iced Teat, and slosh her with frigid water just before leaving for "a show" and her with the job of cleaning it up. Ha Ha.

Ramona is informed that no matter what she can never live in this apartment.Everyone is thanked for taking the time to do whatever they've been doing. Showing the apartment, approving of it, denying the rental. They have all done well. It has been good days work. Ramona sighs and squints fiercely as might a jumper who has set himself to jump over an impossibly high wall. While he looks at the wall, it is the wall he cannot jump, which is impressive to all. Had he ever jumped over well then what kind of wall would it have been after all? What kind of shitty wall can a person jump over who is just a person? But a wall you can't jump over. Well. The whole procedure has made Muffy desperate to move. Simply desperate. Shopping for apartments is just so much fun.

LETTER TO DAD
part 3... graduate school

Muffy has found this magazine for which her father writes. He is talking about something chemistry-ish, something government-ish, something she used to know about, when science was more prominent. It's some sort of smart magazine. Glossy. And all. She tears a piece of paper out of her notebook and lays it on top of the magazine, aligning the first line with his byline. She writes carefully, with a careful cautious pen, as she imagines a huge fan would write.

Dear Dr. Friere,

I am a huge fan. I have been reading your articles for years. I consider myself your mental equal. In fact, I have received many good grades in school. I have a matter of intense intellectual purport that I would like to discuss with you. I have a question which you will find fresh and appealing, and yet which will not threaten you in your mastery of your subject. I wish to engage you in a discussion that is purely impersonal, to assure you that I have no interest in your personal history or your colored past. I have no idea what you have done in your life or who you have abandoned. I am merely a fellow smart person who wishes to converse with you only in writing about topics unrelated to family, fatherhood, and love.

Sincerely,

Muffy Franklin

She persuades Dave to walk her home, saying that she will let down her hair and they can walk around by the lake and possibly get really tanned. Dave goes for this in a big way and even puts his arm around her.

I was thinking about moving, says Dave vaguely, gazing at the camera, which is now hovering apparently somewhere above the lake but not too high. *I'm thinking about... getting away. You know, getting away.*

She nods attentively and already has plans to refer to them as "Dave and I" when talking to real estate agents. She will be silly and only care about the windows and the kitchen counter space and Dave will have to attend to matters like the pet deposit and whether there are adequate outlets in the kitchen for the little wife's hair appliances. He will laugh and the realtor and he will bond over the difficulties of having wives. Wives! Impossible!

Dave walks in a beautiful way, sweeping the other men out of the way grandly with each step. The way they part before him and his cheekbones, she wonders if any of the rest of them have names. These are the men I spend my weeks with, she thinks. Each week another. And then turn them inside out and lay them out to fry because they're done. She doesn't want this beautiful Dave to have to bother with them. She doesn't want them to scuff up his lovely white shoes. She thinks that Dave has a very certain and particular name: Dave. Dave thinks he is more beautiful and Doggydog thinks he is more smart. And so they are. Except that Doggydog just isn't quite so smart as he used to be since he moved in. You can't go around dancing with people who want to dance with you. You have to select the most precious colors in the pile. And where there are forty blues, forty reds, there will be only one green, and you want green the most. Because green doesn't want you. Green thinks you will probably be a lousy roommate. A simple way would be: Will you? Yes. Tis a gift to be simple. And some color-change eggs are special and cause green to turn red with only the heat of a human hand. She doesn't know if Dave will be a good husband or whether she will be afraid. She only knows that his kind of apartment is one she is not likely to get in. *It is dangerous for pretty girls who are interestingly crazy,* says Mrs. Plussize to her in a letter. *There are a lot of men who will suck at you as if with a straw stuck right into your brain. The only people who won't suck your brain are the ones who don't want to suck your brain. Who think your brain is probably better off chloroformed.* Thus spoke Mrs. Plussize, genius of mailboxes.

I really would like to get rid of my current roommate, she says spaciously, *he's brilliant of course, a brilliant and wonderfully talented artist, but the apartment simply reeks of it sometimes.*

Your place smells like cat piss, says Dave. She recalls the time she shoved Doggydog into a roomy closet for the evening and entertained Dave at a frightening level of hysteria, shrieking with laughter to hide Doggydog's mucky guitar noise and claiming to have installed a humidifier in the closet to explain away the wisps of soaked cigarette smoke that escaped under the door.

We don't sleep together in any meaningful way, she explains.

You don't even have a cat, says Dave. *It's more like, if you follow me, the idea of how cat piss smells, there is there, a representation, like if cat piss smelled like a house, and your house was full of cat piss, then there would be a smell, and that smell would be in your house, but without the cat, and without the piss, and then it wouldn't be full of cat piss at all.*

Dave wrestles with the concept of metaphor like a sailor battling a great wind, and with as many piercing stares into the blue yonder as such a sailor could be expected to make in a year, if he kept himself busy staring. Muffy smiles bravely, squinting her eyes in recognition, and thinking about floor tile, how you could choose it and everything.

So do you want to move in with me? she asks.

Interview with Dave:

LJ: Someone of your physical beauty, and your apparent lack of interest in anything but your navel—what are you doing with Muffy?

DM: I'm very busy. It's not in my nature to spend long periods of time on the telephone. I can't do it. You understand. So if I didn't call you, it was because I was busy, and because I don't use the telephone.

LJ: I'm asking you about Muffy. Why did you go out with her?

DM: I dry my face out the window in the morning, and now and then I have a little blower. Towels are terrible for your face.

LJ: The more you speak, the more you become vaguely homosexual.

DM: Muffy is, you know, Muffy is Muffy. What can you say?

LJ: Don't you mean to say, and I know you mean, that she lived in the building next to yours?

DM: So many people have lived near me. It's hard to say.

LJ: And the train was right there beside your building? Remember?

DM: A homosexual man would never live that close to the train, honey.

LJ: And then you would say that she used to get ready for work, and then come out on the back porch, and stick her head out around the building, watching for the train, and as soon as she could see it, or at least hear it loudly, she'd take off running for the station? And

you would declare with a popping vein that you'll
never forget the sight of her streaking down the
alley with her hair flying all over, racing that
train and then you would silently imagine her
pounding up the stairs and onto the platform just
in time, but not share that with me, because it was
just too too precious? Right?

DM: Probably.

LJ: <thinking he **can** contemplate the sublime> Is this
how you look when you stare into the ocean?

DM: I've never been to the ocean. But I do like the
lake.

It'll be nice at the new place, says Muffy, *They'll have
activities for you in the evening and everything and everything.*
Doggydog is fumbling with his file. *I'll be taking my file,* he
says dimly. The folding file looks like it has been chewed by
animals. Doggydog has been moving his belongings around
all day, pointing to the little office loft that he built and
saying *I built that,* and dragging out the little maxipad that
he had written on, saying *I smell Muffy's poo.* He stops by the
mural that he had painted outside the bathroom, a neon
green snake that was supposed to have an elaborate backdrop but he got tired and decided that backdrops were
theoretically capitalist. *I'm not going,* he says suddenly. *And
I'm not staying here either. I'm just nothing. I'm just nothing.* He
starts smoking in the window, pushing at his collar with one
finger, attempting to relieve the itching that the collar
perpetually aggravates on his mangy skin. She thinks that
in the home they will wash his face more than she is able to

manage it. *You've got to go,* she says. *I'm moving in with Dave. I'm not putting on a show for you, woman,* he says.

Muffy calls up Ramona and asks for help in evicting Doggydog. She feels it is too much for her. Ramona arrives on the scene wearing purple overalls and with her greying hair snatched up in a bun. She always chooses glasses with extremely large frames. She says she doesn't want to be looking at plastic when she's trying to merge on the freeway. Surveying the scene, Ramona loudly ascertains that the herd of dorks must be enlisted to remove Doggydog from the scene. They will have to use their faces and their absolute rage against rejection.

LETTER TO DAD
part 4... adulthood

Hey Daddy!
It's me Muffy. Listen, you've GOT to stop calling me all the time! <SENSE OF HUMOR BANG RIGHT OFF THE PAGE> I swear to god if you do not stop interfering in my life I'm going to run away and join the hill people. You raised me with morals and ideals and it's time to let go and let me live my own life. <OH THE BITTER IRONY - GET IT? GET IT?> I know you're just interested in my well being, but come on! Let's try to keep the phone calls down to once a week. It hurts me to say this after you've been so supportive and affectionate over the years. but it's starting to get on my nerves and I just need some space. <HA! HA! HA! FUNNY, HUH?> Thanks Dad..

I love you,
Muffy.

<u>Interview with A Dork:</u>

RD: For the job with the artfuck, we had to really redefine ourselves from *the group of rejected suitors* to *the angry mob*. It is really <chuckling mildly> a small step. The artfuck was firmly entrenched in her life, books mostly, had to be removed. It was hard cleaning the house after him.

LJ: Why do you chase around after Muffy like you do?

RD: REMEMBER THAT REJECTION IS THE ANTIDOTE FOR LOVE. REMEMBER THAT FOR THE LOVE OF GOD. <wildeyed>

LJ: Uh, yes. And Muffy?

RD: <crossing hands pleasantly in lap> She's very very beautiful. And she goes to the most interesting places. She took me to a club once. Of course it's frustrating, never having her call me back. But I like the extremism. She never calls. I never give up.

LJ: What would you do if you saw that she was really interested in you? What then?

RD: Why I don't know. I'd have to get a whole new wardrobe. And that sister of hers. Jesus, what a terrifying hag.

LJ: Do you love her?

RD: Well I don't know, but I can say yes for now. <raising eyebrows gently as if granting favors> Hiffler has this theory, the Pretty Lunatic Theory. Pretty girls who are slightly <wave of the finger toward the forehead> undone, shall we say, get chased by those of my ilk... unfortunates with few social graces and an abundance of quiet time. It's not like they're going to turn around and

actually see you and expect you to buy them a
minivan with a carseat. So you get all the drama
with half the routine. Ho ho.

You piece of crap, shout the dorks waving pitchforks. *I would have been so good for her. Look at MY straw,* some of them say. They squabble and peck at each other but somehow get Doggydog's scrawny limbs out of the house. They transport him to his new quarters at the Home for Ejected Asshole Deadbeats, where volunteers would ponder him and neglect him and listened to his woes and make him get up and make him eat something besides nasty chili that he cooked himself. Volunteers would never long for new frontiers. The dorks stand in a cluster around the door, being sure that he is safely ensconced in his room, with the door shut tightly, before they wander off, turning their attention to Dave.
In her new apartment, Muffy glows with excitement at each expanse of wall. Here for the standing lamp. There for the potted plant. Ramona accuses her of standing on the beach of the promised land. *What now* says Ramona. *You'll only have to look for a new one next year.* She has outlined in black on the floor all the places that Dave probably most wants her to be. She has organized his tennis equipment by age of racket. She has discovered that the camera is now located, by the intensity of his eyes, in the fireplace, and situates herself there often, hoping to intercept his gaze.

Interview with one of the people who got the random
mailings:

LJ: What did you think when you got the random mailing? Were you surprised?

HT: Of course. I almost sent it back. But then I thought, such a thing so rarely happens. I should indulge myself. Be selfish, I thought. Keep it.

LJ: What interested you about the contents?

HT: The letters were fascinating of course, because they showed so much. Really more of her friend in Canada's life, almost a chronicle. But they referred to events and people in Muffy's life as well. Asked questions. There wasn't a diary, and I'm almost glad. That would have been too decadent.

LJ: Did you find yourself wanting more?

HT: The pictures were interesting of course, but I really couldn't tell which one was Muffy. There were three girls that appeared in several shots, in various combinations, and then some men. One man had handwritten an entire blank book full of little poems for her. Terrible writing, probably high school.

LJ: Would you like to meet her, based on these things?

HT: I enjoy meeting people, in general. I find people fascinating.

LJ: Um, yeah. What if you were her father?

HT: Well I expect I'd feel the same way.

Callia the Vallia

not to say cruel sadistic warlike epic godmother of spiderdykes. nor unnaturally vengeful. she meets the enemy on the day of the dead at sunrise in the pittsburgh international airport. standing there waiting because there was no reason not to come back here to the spermatic boyfriend. half asleep outside under the archway outside the international archway waiting for that boyfriend anti-hero to arrive in his chariot with the horses that don't make noise and disappear into mists rolling in tendrils and touching plant stems. plant stems. ooh. but the anti-hero does not arrive. and there is this other man there waiting too.

she says something about horses to the man.

you looked at my boots and you said something about horses because you thought i was a rider and you thought you might be able to sleep with me that way.

that's not true. you can ask my boyfriend she says lighting the cigarette and tossing the match onto the pavement, acting like she was looking for a chariot she knew.

you shouldn't really be smoking should you he says.

what do you mean?

in your <u>condition.</u>

today there was no one to meet her at the airport, imagine, but she met a man who took her to her apartment and fucked her. she had cleaned her house before she left pittsburgh but the house will never be or stay absolutely clean because she is still living in it, the best thing to do is to leave for a while and get away from mother too, she makes Callia so mad, like she would say about the hair dye, *it works really well and look it is so cheap,* implying all these things, what was spent, what should be spent, or she'll point out something in front of a man, the way Callia tears at her nails, *look, your fingers look like little christmas trees.* she still thinks, don't leave the bottles out or the ashtrays or the used pregnancy sticks but her mother hasn't seen a house of hers, oh never, not even dorm rooms, she'll get herself around forever and not need mother to move her here or there, or here's another thing that mother said, when Callia said *i need an exfoliant because down here on my jaw it is rough where i scratched myself,* and she said *well it always used to be that way didn't it,* like she owned it.

the airport man hires her to teach riding lessons at his farm

and still fucking her

his son's name is dale

they are in the dusty riding arena outdors, and she starts picking up rocks and chucking them outside the ring partly to get rid of them and partly to emphasize points in the lesson. the horse is a pony, square, nothing, he has blooded and killed eight foxes, he has been blooded, he has been raced panting through. the yanking going on down in the mouth is tight. the boy's fists are wrapped around the reins and with each rising step a sharp yank on the bit. the horse's mechanical tenseness is clear to her, his clenched tailset and his anchored head, not moving for anything braced.

drop the reins

dry weather for weeks makes the air too hot and the dust rises off mixed in horse crap and dried sand and rocks and flies in the dust are disgusting. trees are covered in it. the arena is raised, cut into the hill above the barn. there could be found no flat land around here western pennsylvania, no one could even have a pool. so for the setting there is a granite mansion at the bottom of the yard, looking sharply down over the river, then the yard and garden carefully planted and the satyrs and monks. the barn is period. oak beams and tiny coach house for hitching, brass handles on all the stalls incantations. the boards on the floor broken up making it hard to sleep but they are solid, as if broken up before or always, cobwebs and handblown glass windows, ancient fires melting and blowing and cursing and being blown. herself, callia the vallia, nut under her back and foot placed on carriage house attic window, takes it in the butt her eyes on god and her hand on her middle, he has thrown her underwear over the rat holes deeply not watching her, and between the hay bales in the old caretaker's apartment up above, under olympic vistas, knife through or pillar through or tree trunk or spear in her. sacrificed. laid out. tackroom full of flies signifying. tired faucets and chewed up buckets with the snaps on the handles replaced with baling twine. stamping hollow sounds hollow in the stalls. it might take more money to maintain this old stable, than to make up a new stable. and less energy.

and more ambiance

he watches her teaching

he does not drag the ring to make it easier to ride there. the anti-hero does not ever arrive in his chariot with his horses that make no noise. she drives out every day from their old apartment now hers to teach lessons in the good country air of the decayed old mansion. to this her new boyfriend? this aged monster? she would lie down and he, the enemy, would put claws all over her stomach making her snake rise up. she says *if my boyfriend were alive he would be dead. if he were in alabama he would be in detroit. if my boyfriend were in tuscaloosa he would be in detroit. and dead DEAD!* rich people bang horses in the mouth like big toothy things. rich people are like that.

the only time she feels perfect is back in the city running in running shoes. out at the farm the enemy has bought her a glorious mount. little mare with no throatlatch, with a short back and tempery face. she loves the mare. and he says to marry him would be her best option. what the fuck does he think. her puking and swelling.

it is hard for her to select
one bridesmaid's dress
with nothing to match it to

after the wedding he takes her inside his house for the first time. always before in the stable, on the hay bales. now into the cavelike lair of the demon, mammon. there the paintings surprise her against the dark wood of the upstairs. the paintings are probably very old unless when she touched them they were wet. or one was. little tiny children in the woods which she almost recognizes as nearby, or at least the winter trees may have looked similar to the summer land-scape. no veil, no train, grassy after the rain, the little mare waiting in the stall with her little hooves and damp fetlocks, receiving hot poultices, receiving selenium and flexfree supplement and manna, restless.

sit back with your shoulders she says up in the riding ring to the student his son dale.

—on the wedding bed of marriage she is pulled over on her back on top of him with her stomach to the painted ceiling and the demon, mammon, can insert himself from behind leaving her free on top to roll—

the boy rolls his shoulder's back impossibly and bounces on the back of the saddle.

—the thrusts of each thrust make her put her butt down into him as one hand on her hip and one on her shoulder keep her there. she can put her head on his collarbone or let it loll off to the side. she cannot touch the bed with her head—

it is not possible to ride this way he says. *i hope you can understand the simple laws of physics. i can't rise over my hips without my body coming forward. my knee is a joint not a hydraulic lift.*

—by bracing her heels down she can wiggle and stay anchored, arching her hips down and hurting her back—

sit back with your shoulders. the horse takes punishment into its big chestnut frame and seems to widen in its bones, seems to get a slimmer head and a longer hip, seems to become a dragon.

other students ride other horses and excel

she had been national champion recently

it's all here every detail is present in the cracks. the housekeeper with her thick ankles and dog, and the bell ropes and carpets red orange fire colored and even the fireplace. the dog lies down before the altar and the fire licks at him. the shadows of fire touch him. except Callia the Vallia not having made or been gifted with any mirror shields or any anklets or even rifle shirts, wears the same everything from her old boyfriend's house in pittsburgh where wadded up sneezerags in the garbage could be used as toilet paper. if this enemy her demon husband, tryst with him, could come home from town with a pile of clothes, embroidered socks, heels, hats, lingerie, but then they wouldn't be her size by the time they got upstairs. having been stretching. she wishes bo the dog would be friendly to her. the enemy in his library reads up on historical facts, like how the mayans used to make certain statues and how the mayans were killed horribly and surrendered or didn't surrender and were killed wretchedly.

she goes toward the quarry to run instead of then the pavement in the city.

running up the steep incline away from the house there are woods and it is not sunny. the berry branches are thinner in the woods and weaker. the ferns twist with wild geraniums around the base of oak and maple which combine their branches far above her head. what combines, mostly fire. what has feet and hair. deer trails cross over the rises and falls down in droppings fresh and shiny, she puts the adidas on either side, with the smell of old leaves and deep deposits of topsoil, mushrooms, the wetness of the stream, and protruding rocks to harbor bear or snakes, the hollowness of the earth under her feet seems to cushion her, each step, unlike cement. unlike dryness. she can smell animals, she smells ferns. it feels high ceilinged and breathable. the stumps have been torn open by ravaging gangs of vandals or merry men and the dark red grain of trees is moistly grubbed. rotting into the ground. she can see a child behind a tree and then running in its white cradle dress to the next tree. it shakes its head at her to make her run faster, laughs and shrieks but she can't hear it. the motion of her running makes trees cross over and separate, turned over branches come into view then hidden, the creek to her left, the creek to her right as the land on one side or the other becomes impassably steep or easy, ferny, and flat. the child is between the combining trees with yellow hair and no sandals and it can keep up with her. it flashes out.

the favorite time is riding out over the grass away from the barn. demon-man, her new husband, keeps his stirrups too high crouched there in a forward seat crosby saddle as if he could lift up and jump the branches and bushes himself. he is so challenging it burns her at the skin. the mare is hotter to keep up than she is, little bunched up flanks under her, so quick, to get ahead of the big black gelding horse, for a couple strides. she won't take the bit, she just tucks her head in farther and lunges. she is afraid to let her out and pass the gelding. and the mare is also terrified of this. he the leader races over no path and the road opens up. and he turns left.

and the mare darts left

she falls into the ditch with the stirrup undone

the mare stops still

she is crouched in the ditch next to a rock and a little pond of rain water. the scrying pool and rhymes lie just under her eye. her hand is under her side, she fell off at right angles. she can't breathe or feel if there is any pain. the nice handsome man swings his reins over a low branch and the black horse sidesteps to hear the clattering mare down the hard dirt road.

i'm pregnant she says immediately

divorce me she says

he picks her up and makes her stand up on the high bank while he puts his hands all over her. the clay and scrubby weeds sticking out of the bank brush against the front of his plastic demon suit as he leans. a trickle fills the rain pond and a trickle spills over down the hill. in her bed the doctor's long black coat and spectacles. they must be far away from everyone to have a doctor like that. had she noticed, driving here, or was it too far away to drive to? in her bedroom on her bed where she will stay for eleven weeks, she hears them.

will the child live?
yes there is no damage
keep her quiet
keep her eating

she: i dream about slipping through the door crack to where he is sleeping in his room. i lie above him and press my rib cage and hip bones into him, and i make him scream how hard i can eat his balls and how much i can lick him. his bed has a thick cover which absorbs the screaming and the walls are thick. i eat up the jism so it can go down and make the baby his baby instead of my boyfriend's. at least it can be nourishing. when he is lying there with his face and body covered up i can go downstairs and run. so that the baby is taken care of. so that i can live in a mansion and say glorious things. so that one day this will all be yours. and out into the woods. at night i am afraid of bears. i tell the little child in the woods that he is mad at me i lied to him and hid that i was pregnant. the child runs around me staying between the trees and i sit against the elven throne made by a stunted tree scuffing and making piles in the pine needles.

you didn't tape your stomach down
you didn't wear anything
he knew when he put his hand on
he loves that baby is not his
    when she can get out of bed she is still stopped from
going to the barn or to town or to pittsburgh. Callia the
Vallia his penis in her arse. Callia the Vallia body getting
warse. tumdilly deedle doo oink oink tiddle, she thought.
there are bars rising up around her when she would want to
walk forward. she takes a step and judges if the bars could
be leaped. but if that could have been done, even with the
flying shoes, she would have been speared through the
body as they rose up faster to meet her. at last the bars got
so close and obsessed with her that she had to pee in her bed
and the wet dripping down in hell made him mad. she can't
go putting out the fires beneath with her lazy pee. each time
she tries to sleep the bed begins to fall out from beneath her
leaving her gripping the nose of the dead horse over the
headboard. his stuffed head is black and his hard nostrils.
    after the baby is born she can do anything she wants so
she goes out to the barn. the only same thing is her mare
who is thinner and tired. big black horses are in all the stalls
with hairy fetlocks and heavy jaws, they keep their eyes shut
and feel their ways around the stalls by memory or intu-
ition. the barn has sprung to heroic proportions. she sits
against the door of her horse's stall, softly, keeping her pussy
off the floor. he won't fuck her now probably. the only
important thing is the baby. so once she gets over this sore
it will be the last sore. if she had the baby with her instead
of with the housekeeper, she would also have a rocking
chair. in the aisle over the broken floorboards she would

have a tiny blanket and a flannel nightgown. slippers. tinkling sounds of a music box piped into the barn as she rocks the baby and sings whispering and whimpering along. all the horses would gather round as in most nativity scenes, these big black blind horses a round swinging light descends from the ceiling such as comes into most detective movies, and circles around her light up on the floor.

she could read

walk around

ride

while asleep her husband in a tuxedo enters her room and asks her to go into town. he puts a hand over her eyes and says

wouldn't you like to go and see your mother.

a tickle of worry begins to molest the bottoms of her feet and she kicks off the covers and sits up to see him. he looks weird. either he has gotten very very old without it being apparent in his face, or his clothes are not made of anything organic. she forgets to answer him while she remembers this was what he wore to marry her, before the horns and other eye came out on his head.

no

we're hosting a few guests.

downstairs every light is excited.

each guest has smooth skin and quiet eyes, and each face has been smiling and talking for two hundred years. the rustle of heavy skirts skips over carpets and wood floors, glasses crash against each other and stay whole. she sees the doctor that delivered her baby. what could she possibly put on her body or do to her face that would allow her to come to the party. the women are wigs, the men are wifes, the children snarl at each other and turn their lips down, buckle boots and knee socks ribbed and clotted. her grey t-shirt has been worn by the old boyfriend and has had the neck stretched out. her shorts barely reach her knee without fringing off. she finds her slippers and goes out to the barn across the dark lawn through the window frames lit up on the grass.

the little mare no shoes turned out in the paddock
have they been starving you she says
it is dangerous to ride on the trails at night
when they are out there they just walk. for hours. they look continuously up to the sky to see comets, and Callia shouts out *no deer anywhere near* in a singsong voice to make the deer spook and get out of the way, to prevent the horse from being alarmed, an antler in the face. oil wells working click up and down in the dark with little children riding them like seesaws, each baby girl in a white dress, the tired little thin horse pricks her ears back and forth, not wanting to see them. what happened to his ex-wife anyway. and was there a child a baby sister. Callia spots the circle of evil through the trees and a baby crying being forcibly held. where is her baby. she kicks her heels into the little dead mare's sides and manages to work up a trot. she should have been fed and brushed and had her hooves picked out daily. as the trees cross and uncross it becomes clear that a group of the party guests have decided to ride out in black robes, their white hair shines on top. a fire burns inside the circle of them lighting up the baby in his arms, he is wearing a mask that is shaped like his face and sits on the biggest horse. these eyes are open and red and runny. which had been blind. words are being spoken as she draws nearer, and

knives are being raised by the party guests.

she yells out his name and they turn their heads
on her grey unfancy little horse
and her hair in a ponytail

they have no intention of stopping until she kicks the horse into a canter and breaks in next to the fire sitting there staring. her mare gives over to the other horses and is rooted. her husband with his big arms and legs, black boots to his thigh and belt catching the rough robe around his waist seems attractive with his ugly head. if she could have been timely she would have a gun. if she were taller she would be able to ally with the baby, if allied then better horse, if better horse than wild escape.

why did you think i married you he says

my sister says the boy dale chanting and pointing to the children like ghosts which are now gathered in the trees. they have nothing to say to her. the demon lord mammon gives her the child to hold and the party guests arrange in formation around her like a pointed star all horses facing one way and then they start moving and the biggest knife is in her back. they will be skewed on the same knife the baby on her shoulder. *what are you fucking sick* she says. she imagines herself as her part in this lively ritual, the baby, they must have been doing it. what happened to the boy Dale's mother for god's sake. did they pour her blood on her older son or the then baby's blood to sacredize him or to initialize him. did the mother die was not the foremost question in her mind. they have moved into a canter seeming to ride straight through trees and she can see they mean to drive on although the mare is dead or dying. she stumbles, her weak hips slanting down and she falls though

pricked and bitten by the redeyed monsters on each side.
    Callia the Vallia not as high
    standing straddling her dead mare as she heaves
    the arms around the baby
    then through the night comes a slight ruffle and immediately though late for the airport comes the antihero ultraman virgin-buster boyfriend. in his chariot and horses that don't make any noise on the ground, through the mist, he has been the surprise of the evening before. she is jerked by the force of his grip and the baby gets snatched by the arm yanking them into the chariot. *take me* she says. falling into the back, gilt edge coming up to meet her face and head hurting. turning on one wheel as in tricks, the boyfriendman plunges through the circle of horsemen and party guests his bold noble face etched against the backdrop of evergreens and his hands sensitive on the reins, two chestnut geldings perfectly strided. back to the fire. pursued by the ponderous and long black horses and the demon man in front is expressionless and throwing knives in a steady rhythm. ultraman whose baby is now nuclear reaches a torch into the demon ritual fire and it flares mighteously in the hand. he clucks to the horses and begins a figure pattern, pulling the pursuers together and torching one tree and the next which light up toward the sky, spreading the fire to the house and housekeeper, to the river, the horsemen slowly and luxuriously turn and turn writhing throught the predicted pattern serpentine, flying leads on the straight line, halt and back, traverse, piaff, shoulder in.
    hot wind in her hair and her face
    his arm around her ribs
    triumphant on the road

Prison Tits

The year was bad for romance, and the cellmates dreamed of steam rising in pillars from the prison, columns they could see from their homes seventy miles away. *Fuck you Maurice,* said Lora, *I'm out of here for good.* Seven years of Lora's memories were clear, and then she saw them fading. First with the names, then the eye color — maybe hazel, maybe grey. If she tried to hurt or kill him, it had nothing to do with his life. It was the prison that she couldn't bring back right. It was that woman. *Remember the one thing that you can still think about,* she said, *the one thing you just know for sure was not somebody else's life?* But Maurice had never recovered from a fat childhood. His chest bone stuck out beyond his hips, and his navel was a horror. He would never even be okay, though he tried many different ways. Was he a nice guy? Could he ever really be a nice guy? Lora on the phone, to a dishwasher and an ex-con, that was the woman. *Maybe Oregon,* she said to her, *I haven't got a lot of money. Maybe Washington.* The voice of the phone said, *Who is this again?* From that prison at Jackson Michigan they had driven away seven years ago. They didn't write. Or call. They had dreams about bondage and got all aroused at the thought of metal. They wore blue a lot, and that wasn't normal. The cell where they lived was still in the prison, with some new people in it. Lora started the car she had stolen from Maurice just then, and pulled out of the Quikmart across the street from their house. He was in the window, but the door stayed slammed. Grey eyes or hazel, underarm hair growing upwards or down, in a swirl? Brush your hair forwards first? Wipe your ass from the front or back? *Well okay, why don't you just start your own little goddamn society,* said Maurice. Lora tapped the wheel and repeated to herself a snatch of dialogue because the more she thought about memory, the more the litany was reduced to the picture without the sound or vice versa. She could hear Ginny with a stick face or see her with a stick voice. She drove faster and treated the car really bad. *The only real meadows are in England,* she thought about if Ginny would remember saying that and knew there were probably sixty other things she would rather remember. If Ginny would remember the sixty other things then it would be worth it. But her stupid job stocking produce — anything would be more important than showing up for work. Just to discover a clean rest stop on the way to her mother's house would beat that with one leg caught in a jock strap. Lora yanked her hair into the pony tail band she kept around her gear shift. It was one she had lifted off a sweet girl at the market who loaned everything out. That girl didn't have a sharp enough eye to check over lettuce, so she stacked or she stood around and tried to marry the customers. Lora had an exacting eye for detail. Lora was a pick pocket, in the market, at the city bar, in the clean rest stops. But she had asked for the pony tail holder, to see if the girl was really that stupid. How long had they been in there pouting before the prison conversation regressed to looks and murmurs, and how had Ginny asked for soup without so many noodles? And got it.

Ginny was too perky and as they lay there at night they had set up thieving rackets in their minds thinking they would have her act as a distraction — to use the perkiness. She might even go down on the men turning their heads so Lora could steal the money. She might talk about it for hours after dark when Lora just thought about Maurice. Mean thoughts, along with the humming fantasies of the younger girl below her in the bunk. Or if she had been on the bottom bunk, then the hand that fell over the side with fingers. *Find your own bondage and get to know it,* said her mother laughing. To mothers, pickpockets make great conversation, unless the pickpocket is in jail and there is no smoking in the visitation room, and no big armchair to hold the spreading body, no skillets and onions to splash with wine. In which case the mother becomes concerned in the usual ways, about health suddenly, and reads scripted conversations, too nice, which might give Ginny the wrong idea. *She's not like that,* said Lora anxiously, *at home she's a real dragon.* As long as the lines of Ginny's jaw were more familiar, and as long as a peek over the bedside was rewarded by the sleeping sight. She stepped on the gas and fingers shaped out that quiet girl everyone warned her about. *She's a real downer what you want is somebody older because she looks alright but oh I've heard some stories. It's just like a fit, like some kind of seizure.* Who had she taken off with, was it Jerry or Samuel or had she called him Mr. Something — awful. Lora's feet had been inside the jail but the rest of her stretched out, stood up out the top, heard the laughter hitting out of the car and saw the pony tail pulled. Ginny had not told her about what murder for a long time. Then it was the night in February when everyone had been pissy and Ginny laughingly recalled the satisfaction of knifing someone, how it had been so easy and really a learning experience. *Shut your fucking mouth,* said Lora, *and maybe you won't be in here your whole fucking life.* They had worked it out, Ginny and this lover, and her dead husband had come at her, too violent anyway. Everyone knows about mitigating circumstances. She had only lived seven years in prison, but it was all a very exciting education, apparently. And what was said? And now that she was out? Now she and shithead were living in what paradise? Lora gripped the wheel, thought of all the pissant towns and each of them had ended up in a really fine situation. Both of them dying their hair on the same night, as a special. They sat on Ginny's bed and wrapped a towel around her shoulders first, and poured on the cheap black dye, giggling as if they had someone in there with them. Neither wanted a hair cut, and Ginny's red and thick hair took two bottles of gel, while Lora's was too dark to really see a difference after they washed it out. They lay in the same bed, and Lora smoothed the cellmate's hair over the white sheets and cried over it, more because they had been happy. Ginny wanted to look scary, she wanted to defy the people. Lora wanted to bring back the shiny golden hair. Ginny lost too much weight and used body lotion for once. It didn't make her better, it just brought what color to her face, not the right kind. The cellmates knew they were beautiful in that their own cell, even after the dyes, and even years later they did it again because the hair never came back quite as nice. Well they would write movies, they would star in great films, they would become columnists in teen magazines because anyone could do that, they would run for office because someone should do that, all and all they would do as soon, the moment they could get out of that cement grey atmosphere. They held each other's hands after what nightmares. They counted all the bricks in their walls just to get that over with. They had a plan for every night, as if they could ward something off that way. To look forward, to look around, to want out, they may have been denying or pretending, Lora now told herself. She never could remember solid details even in prison. *But,* she said, *how could I have forgotten the air out here and how absolutely every day seems to end and the hordes and hordes of people that are just as good as me.* Lora made plans for what she would say when she saw the girl again. Now they could really go because they had a car, and they could do anything. Fuck the wrinkles. Maurice was responsible anyway and all his shitty compliments. *Listen,* she said aloud in her car, *I just want to let some people know they're really appreciated.* She could have wished for a different car. She would have painted this one white instead of dark blue, but she wasn't trying to escape recognition. She drove this car to work every day. Now she had stolen it and she wasn't any farther away than normal. Some things were different, like her clothes in the back seat or the radio off, would tell someone she was gone for good. But if she washed the car or painted it white? *There's Lorry Stone drivin' around in someone else's car.* She would drive to Algonac where Ginny worked in a restaurant. She had made special efforts to track down a work number. Didn't want to call her at shithead's place. He was always shithead no matter who he was. Would the girl rather go to the West or the East? Would she have a better car that they could use? Lora began searching the sides of the road she was driving on, a wide shouldered lake road, with fishing tackle stores along both sides. Cory Ann's was the name of it, out past the ferry to Walpole Island. She passed the ferry. The girl had spent seven months in the city of London, where she met what husband who she had killed. In this time she worked in the Mews, shoveling shit for the Queen and wiping off the endless equipment, harnessing and exercising the warmbloods and hackneys. Lora had known all the names of the horses because it was a fond memory and they often went over it. Ginny touched and cleaned the great gold that carried the married couples in the family, that sat in the shaded sun for tourists. It was hard to clean, and it had a secret ugly chip that she hadn't told anyone about. Under the hub on which rear wheel was this tiny little chip. Lora smiled and choked at the thought of little Ginny. What secret had they pulled up about the prison. She spotted a sign that said Cory Ann's and took in the sight of the place, the gravel parking lot, the screen door. *She's not here,* said the bearded man in a maroon booth seat. *Went home sick - she lives out toward St. Clair though, turn right at that stoplight a ways back and keep on that there. It's a little white farm about six miles west. Got a big fucking dog house.* Lora let her breath huff out of her as she slammed the door. Maroon seats and a tile floor, half empty ketchup bottles with crap around the lids. She imagined Ginny with her sparkling hair and her trim waist and smooth knees, in a boardroom or checking over proofs for some magazine or riding horses in perfect hunting clothes. Maybe they could go to night classes or something. She sped down the road and passed several white farm houses before she saw what could be a shed or a dog house in front of a one storey house with a covered porch. She saw a fine big dog emerge from the shed and pulled into the driveway. The dog bounded over to her car as it came to rest and the engine stopped. He looked in at her and did not bark or move. She beeped the horn and the dog raised his chin stiffly, the whites of his eyes showing as he peered down at her over his lifted nose. *Hey boy how's the wife,* Lora glanced toward the house and garage. A little kid with short red hair went between the two buildings in a tight baby dress, her legs skinny and her arms close to her sides. The dog looked to the house as the door opened again, and a woman stepped out onto the porch, not very tall and slightly heavy around the hips and thighs. She wore a sweater that was not buttoned around her throat but pulled tight around her waist. Lora's knees pushed against each other and she bit at her lips. *Masher,* called the woman and the dog ran to her side. Lora opened the car door and put her ugly black flats on the gravel driveway. The woman's hair was bright and red and fell down to her waist, drawn back from her fullish face with a black ribbon. It was golden against the white of the house and Lora nearly wanted to hold the heap of it in her lap. *Please come in,* said the woman as she neared the porch. Lora reached out a hand and Ginny took it politely. *Let me get you a chair, isn't it funny, that prison.* When she came to the word prison she dropped her voice down as if she had never said fuck. The woman that was Ginny brought glasses of water and lamented that so much time had passed without them visiting. *But I left my husband,* said Lora, *and this is not a visit—like I said on the phone.* Ginny said that marriage counselling had done her husband a world of good and really he was behaving like a perfect gentleman lately. The child came in and bumped against the knees of her mother, and the woman put out a casual hand to touch it. There was a picture on the wall of the child at school, and what looked like a family portrait shot cheaply at the local mall. Shithead was light skinned and had good teeth. The backdrop showed a Christmas tree and a fireplace with a brass grate. Lora drank her water and tried to make eye contact. That woman sat in a light blue armchair and sighed, saying she had wanted to come home today anyway when Lora called, and Dan hadn't been mad because it was pretty slow. *And the baby-sitter got to go home early too,* she said, as if Lora's arrival was just a godsend in every way. Lora sat on one of the straight backed chairs and held her empty glass, felt her dark hair hanging lank around her ears. She was invited for dinner, but Ginny would have to go to the market and get another pork chop. *Although Sherry never eats her whole chop,* she said, *but we'll get a nice dessert, too.*

Beating Faces

Jennifer goes to bed early on Friday because the night before, they used the purple condom from the bathroom at Oliver's, and it broke. *Latex,* he said after he tossed himself across the bed, *La—tex.* He has an umbrella and she doesn't, so she's sick when she comes home from work and goes to bed early on Friday without saying goodnight. When she puts her head against the pillow she tries to sleep, and she keeps thinking about if she and Joe would be anything like parents, which would be what happens when a condom breaks. She's whatever — obsessing. Still she doesn't take sinus medication, not even aspirin. Then she thinks about what must be happening. He comes to bed and says, *I'm sorry, I'm so very sorry, I really feel bad, I'm sorry, I'm terribly sorry, God I'm so sorry, sorry, sorry, I'm sorry, I'm completely, utterly, thoroughly, absolutely, totally sorry, I'm so sorry, I feel so bad.*

Jennifer and Joe have conversations that end abruptly because they are on the train and they use different stops. There's time after Joe gets off for Jennifer to think out what she would have said if he hadn't stood up just then, in the middle of his own sentence. She thinks of it. At the corner above Jennifer's stop is a man playing violin, and she thinks it is Joe in disguise, but he's too dirty, and Joe got off the train at Washington Street after all. He's playing and Jennifer drops a train token in his case because she doesn't have any change. She works in a store at a computer that catalogs books and makes enough to really buy an umbrella if she could remember to. The dirty man with the violin doesn't look or smile, so Jennifer's eyes tense up and she taps away in her scuffy blue heels, swearing not to be nice anymore.

Jennifer is so pale, says Joe, *She's so creamy white soft cloudy pale.* Joe is smoking marijuana with his mother. His mother has money. *She has the blackest blackest hair, like shiny thick hair. It's so smooth. She has red nails like drops of paint on a tile floor, she has a pink petal soft—* *Don't tell me about that,* says his mother without moving toward him, *that dowdy bitch has you tied up. You're all tied up.* His mother is sprawling in a black cotton armchair with one leg thrown over the side. She is wearing red leather pants and her hair is straight blonde. *Joe, you've got to keep track of things, hunt her down at work once or twice, bring her a sandwich, get things back in your own front yard.* Joe reaches over and and traces on the wet cold glass by his side, making it dribble on the wooden table. He puddles it with his finger and stretches his neck back and forth. His mother is old, but good at plans. *I'll tell you what,* he says over the loud clock, *If she opens the gate on anyone else's picket fence, she'll get her lawn mowed right down to the dirt.* He moves his feet back and forth on the carpet which looks bad and needs to be replaced. *Stupid,* she says, *You're stupid.* He takes a drag and puts his wedding ring finger in her face. *That's stupid?* he laughs, *Is that a ring or not?*

In high school, Jennifer looked good in the orange gym uniform, pounding around the track in the cold morning, while the blondes were washed-out and the redheads tried to wear black turtlenecks underneath, even in hot weather.

She didn't blush at the boys playing football, and they never whistled because they wanted her too much, so they whistled at the ugly blonde with the little butt, and when Jennifer ran by they threw the ball hard and found excuses to hit each other. There was a boy who didn't like football, and he was the only one who wouldn't play, so he couldn't grunt or scrape for her and he only stared. He didn't want to break his fingers. She ran cross country and he couldn't rate her so he didn't try.

Jennifer puts on white stockings and blue skirts to work. When she passes him on the corner, she pulls her coat tight around her so he can't see. *Joe is a weird guy,* she says to her boss at the bookstore, who listens a little bit. *So what are you saying, you don't like him anymore?* says the boss. *No, but he calls me and doesn't say it's him when I'm home alone, he says it's Angelo or something, and talks like it's some other guy. Then he'll come home and say — Oh, I'm a rapist, and you can't do anything about it.* The boss looks directly at her and sneers. *Slimy fucker trying to trick you into fucking someone else. I bet he wears seventeen layers so you can't really see his body.* Jennifer nods and the boss goes back toward the register, but Jennifer follows her. *No, it's really romantic — I mean he's seducing me... Yeah right, you're going to get stuck with him if you're not careful, you're going to get knocked up and then where will you be?* She knows about it, Jennifer thinks, she must know about that broken condom. She sits down quitely, not to break anything, not to shake her stomach around, and not to make anyone hear her. Seven people come into the store, men and women with one extra man who wants a book about making bread, and has delicate fingers. She could run faster than this man. Her sweater might be tighter today. It might be PMS at last. The man says, *Welcome to my place, welcome to this restaurant, welcome to the place I thought about you in when I was twelve, this is where I held my first hand, this is where the rattle comes from at night, here is the window, my friends call me Trent, my friends call me Sport, it's a long way down don't you think, and you live on the eighteenth floor, nineteenth, you should see the back of my neck, it's thick, here's a picture of what I want to look like, here's another possible look for me, where did you say you lived, is it far, is it far?*

Do you want some more coffee? she asks him slowly. *No, that's okay. I don't want to have to pee all night.* Joe stretches and lets his hand touch her as she goes back out to the kitchen. *Sold any classics? any Dickens?... Why can't you get past Dickens, you know, there's a few things I want you to read, before I'll call you my husband.* He is standing behind her at the sink, where it is easy to put his arms around her because she's not looking. *You know I still think you're afraid of me... You always say that as if you came from a den of drug addicts.* He raises his eyes behind her head and keeps holding on to her as she sloshes water into the frying pan. She says that his mother is okay, really, and she doesn't know what he's worried about because he has a good job, right? *You're very funny,* says Jennifer, turning to face him, *and you know what I'm talking about... What? What's so funny?... You know... Oh sure, if I know then how come I don't know?* Jennifer turns out the light in the kitchen and pulls him on the floor. Might as well, now.

In high school, Jennifer sang in the choir with the boy who stared at her. He talked to her about music, and told her some things about the orchestra, most of which she forgot. He said she should play clarinet because it was an alto voice, like hers. She had always wanted to play the flute, but she didn't argue with him, mostly because she didn't like him. Jennifer's locker partner was in love and she was dying to be in love, and she wanted to get married before her parents made her go to college. She knew that all the girls who played clarinet were strong-minded, and that flute was more lady-like. The clarinet girls had thicker thighs. Jennifer wanted to fall in love with her history teacher, who was too old, or her brother's friend Todd, who was too tall. At homecoming she wore dark blue satin and everyone raved and said she should be a model. She liked the attention, but wished that she could fall in love with her date, who was too skinny. The boy who stared went to homecoming and you'd think he'd come without a date, to see how he never noticed the brain strain he brought to the dance. He came up to Jennifer and said, *Hi — it's Tim from choir?* She went home with the skinny guy from history class and wished it were the teacher, didn't let him touch her breasts but played with his belt very seductively. She went home and her parents were happy to see her, and took pictures again just like before she left. Her father worked the camera and her mother fixed her hair, and then they all had coffee together, and it was the first time Jennifer had ever made coffee, and she felt old.

She kissed him, she kissed his mouth, she let him touch her naked waist, she put her lips against his neck, he fought through her teeth, he held his hand still in her hair, he found out what she was giggling about, she told him, she touched him, she took him, he had his chin on her forehead, they tumbled around, they spilled the glass of water, she held him, she knew he was there, he held her. She is sitting at the kitchen table with the instructions for the pregnancy test, which she has already read five times, and listens partly to the TV, and partly reads the instructions again. *You can finally be sure,* she reads aloud, *with Quick Response.* She looks at the bathroom door where the test is developing and feels like smacking herself, or the door, or running around the block for twenty minutes, or having a child within the next few months, or waiting five years, and she puts her head down, breathing slow. *It's not like a crisis,* she says. The kitchen table is not wood, but dark formica that looks like wood, and it has a napkin holder that also holds the salt and pepper shakers. It has a few papers from Joe's briefcase and all the parts of the pregnancy test instructions laid out in a row. She has not peed directly on the strip, maybe, or maybe she has touched the strip with her finger, or maybe she has left it in too hot a place. There are a lot of reasons why it could be positive that aren't even a problem at all. She should just go in there and pick up the test with her eyes closed, put it in the garbage, keep the top closed and bring it out to the kitchen, all with her eyes closed, put on the twist tie and march it right out the dumpster. Then she could cover it up with a bunch of smelly trash so she won't go out there in the middle of the night and dig it up. She looks at the bathroom door and feels sure she is pregnant. She looks at the TV and feels sure she is not. She looks at the bathroom door.

Is that you are you in there? You're scrambling, but you're not going to leave through the window, you're not leaving. Your address, your phone number, I'm coming, I'm coming, it's not okay to leave shit lying around, it's not safe if anyone knows, you stay home, you scramble for a better lock or door, you separate everything out, yours, his, you hold onto your waistline and your best products, you lay yourself out and ask them to come, well I'm coming. She is really sick now and with Joe gone for the weekend she is left with two dogs. One is hers, Holly, and the other one Punky belongs to the couple downstairs. She thinks all day that Punky will never lie down. He just keeps on humping, trying to get Holly in a good position, but Holly is not interested in sex, seems like the only place they can play is right on her legs under piles of comforters, with her lying there cold. It's a heavy mattress on the floor, and the fourth day of bronchitis is headed into pneumonia maybe, and the cough medicine is laced with codeine. Maybe she'll get good karma back from letting Punky stay, but he has shit on the floor, barfed on the tile, pissed on the couch. Thinking about this makes her moan around while the dogs don't stop slobbering and growling at each other. She yells at the dogs one time and spills them onto the floor by kicking. She's too sick and the only man around is the one across the hall, who Joe hates. She doesn't look nice, and her dark circles are more green than blue.

It's dark and Punky is standing on her chest and glaring. He is the ugliest dog, all terrier cockawhatsit, wiry snotty face and beard. It's obscene the way he gets off on Holly's haunch even, and his spiked collar could be a wristband. She sits up and dumps him off her meanly, they have to go for a walk now. Sweaters, hat, scarf, boots with wool down in them, Punky crouches by the door threateningly. Punky poops this way — leg lifted up to pee, then the poop comes out his doughy little butthole and falls off to the side while the leg is up. His tail was never cut off, but Jennifer would like to, could easily do it, this weekend even. They walk in a hurry and the dogs pull her. A few people are still out under

165

the orangey street lights. An old woman is on the steps of the public pool. She points at Holly and *Is that a beaver?* Jennifer can't stop laughing and that makes her cough, but she coughs out, *No it's a hound. It's a foxhound* while being pulled on down the street. *I meant beagle,* says the woman, *I meant to say beagle.* At home the man across the hall comes to see if she's all right without Joe there, and she wishes she looked better, but Joe tells her to stay home when she's sick, she looks so sallow. Maybe if she weren't pregnant she would take some antibiotics, or if she were pregnant she would get that glow about her. The neighbor talks until the phone rings and he says, *There's someone to cheer you up right now* and she says *Yeah, probably Joe* and is surprised at how caustic it sounds coming out of her mouth. But it's not Joe.

It's wonderful, you shouldn't have, I didn't, it's not your handwriting, is this the place, where is she, after seven years she looks just, why didn't you say it was you, I would have let you right in, oh there you are, thanks, Yes I admit a little weight around the waist, is that a woman, it's that woman, that one there, It's not that I meant to trick you, I'll buzz up and give you the magic secret password, it's here between my, what did you say you were drinking tonight, it's not your hand, it's bigger than that, it's not time yet. When Joe comes back she has a suitcase ready for the hospital and Joe asks her what the fuck is up, and if he did something, could she please tell him? She laughs, *I know it's eight months away, but I'm nervous tonight* His jaw drops and he's holding her close to him, still stuck in his face saying *Why didn't you tell me... I thought you knew, remember you said when the time comes or whatever that was?... I wasn't talking about that... Don't try to scam me, you know what I'm referring to... We have to get you to a doctor... I thought you KNEW about this — wasn't that you?* Maybe he thinks she's just raving, but he tries to forget about it and she can't think about it, whatever he wants is okay right now, even the fantasies. They sleep together, and she doesn't dream about anything, but he dreams about her and her child. He dreams they look almost the same and that he takes the daughter to kindergarten and she hangs back and he can't leave her. He finds it normal that he should dream about it. Perhaps he had known already, because they had worried about it so much, it was bound to happen. She won't go to work the next day, and she won't see a doctor or take any pills. *If you die of pneumonia what then?* Joe is being reasonable. *Pills kill babies and make them have eleven fingers. Punky is gone I can finally get some sleep.*

It kind of creeps her out so the next day she decides. She's never known how to handle Joe's fantasies, except straight on, like when he wants to pretend that she can't speak the language, or when he wants to dress like a construction worker. It isn't that she doesn't have fun, it's just her chest hurts but whatever. They are there, which is up some stairs and she is on the couch, writhing out of her clothes in the dark while he's in the other room. She groans a little to herself, in preparation. Then he is on top of her and the chest touches her naked breasts and she clutches him close and then looks up straight into the face. He bends his knees and crouches down away from her, and it's cold for her lying there. He looks between her legs as if there would be a label, he's reading it, like how does my fingerprint fit into this picture, then his eyebrows unwrinkle. She hasn't opened her eyes in minutes. *There's nothing in there of yours,* she says, which makes him sneer in the dark. *Mine,* he says, *is not in there anyway.* He is too hard, she is too small, they have waited a long time, he won't wait, he won't tell her, she smells that the place is musty and old, and the sofa she is lying on has mothy holes, and he's not a gentleman exactly. He isn't Joe today, but she says the name anyway, as if hoping, and he presses his face into her white neck and moans, and she is too small and he is too hard.

In high school, Jennifer always pictured that it would be quick, one thrust and there — what could take so long? Girls said it was not so great, they watched each other's faces in the bathroom mirrors for possible flaws or mismatched eyeliner, and nobody wanted to like sex too much. Jennifer wore her hair down when she wanted to look older, or for the dance line tryouts she wore it in a braid. Her locker partner wore her boyfriend's brown and gold leather jacket and the hairs that fell out of her when she brushed in the bathroom stuck into the material, so the boyfriend didn't want it back which was okay. Jennifer wanted a boy's class ring so she could wind black thread around it and make it fit her little fingers. She wanted her face to be in someone's head as he rushed down the soccer field, or football, whatever. Permanent, her face. The way it looked right after that single blow, when all of her came out her eyes, he would remember, he wouldn't forget. She could picture it, like the photo of after the homecoming dance, when she realized about dancing and hip motion. Jennifer wanted her picture in someone's locker. Yeah, that's my girlfriend they would say off hand. They would assume it. They would tell their friends about her and how she looked without pants if they ever got that far. Jennifer ran circles around the track and the boys all had their fingers ready.

The Stamp Letters

There's this thing where she gets so restless in her body, not that she has to crack her neck or scratch, although that helps, but there's something that doesn't go right, doesn't feel okay, very horribly unsettled. It's down in her spine or her esophagus. When she was younger and in bed at night she used to kick and bounce around like she was possessed and it wasn't that, it was just this thing. Her mother used to scream at it to stop, yell at her *stop jumping lie down why are you doing that,* and Julie would let a little spit come out the corner of her mouth and she'd be flailing around and really couldn't stop then, because nothing would have changed but she would still have to explain to her mother what changed to let her stop. It got out of control. *Fix it* she's screaming to her mother, and her mother raises up one hand to beat her down, raises and raises and never hits hits hits so that Julie could lie down and be still. The mother never hits her down so she doesn't have to jump around and kick her legs and flail. Just stands there and strains at her face, trying to make an expression. Just her arm going up. Up.

She writes a stamp letter to explain.
Dear mother, it says, *I am writing to explain the situation*

with my sorority pledge party. I pledged. We sang songs that rhymed all the way through and we (littles) had to wear the same dresses that they (bigs) wore, with matching stockings. The stockings were pink, with a seam. I just wanted to thank you for the opportunity to get an education and better myself in this very important way. And impress everyone at work. Love, Julie.

The stamp letter fits on the back of a stamp. On the sticky part you lick it and then hide it away underneath. The stamp letter goes on a sympathy card to Aunt Martha, and she mails it.

At the sorority party Julie comes in naked. The party is in the downstairs of their house which is on campus and no one else can come into it unless they're a friend of yours. At the party there are a lot of friends and a few alumni, and Julie's big isn't pretty drunk she's very drunk. Upstairs in their room Julie is getting ready and putting on a lot of makeup and she has perfect hair and shoes to match, you know, pink, but no dress or even stockings so there's the bruises right there. On her way down the stairs she doesn't visualize any symbolically blooming flower which is blooming just like her life or any other circular type symbol, she just forgets about how she'll be yanked by the ass out of the sorority tomorrow, and all the alumni's faces, seeing her body and what's there, no one is more surprised than they are, the stupid reactionaries, isn't it what they always wanted to do? Get attention.

There is no dream-like atmosphere anywhere as she drifts through the room, there is no memorable suspension of time while everybody stops and looks at her, no halo-esque light setting, nothing like this, in fact she makes it to the bottom of the bannister and then someone, her big, comes up to her laughing and takes her around the wrist hard enough to hurt and jerks her around the corner. Now believe that she has a beautiful narrow frail-boned body and a face that is beguiling and she's cold up against the hand towel rack, starting to be cold, with that peon glaring at her and wanting her to tell about how she had come up with this joke and to smile and tell about the joke and then they would kind of hug but keep their bodies away from each other and then get a towel wrapped around her and go upstairs. The girl would let Julie borrow one of her hair bows but not any of the really nice ones because Julie was probably getting kicked out and why she probably wouldn't even get it back. The big is wanting and expecting all of these things.

She wants to write a quick stamp letter to explain this, scribble it down right beside the sink shaped like a shell, but she can't so she gets axed from the sorority and moves to the city and starts doing phone sex full time, and the line is for lesbians, and she has an excuse to quit school. She would be embarrassed.

She runs the water in the tub and then goes out into the other room. Hears the water splashing in to fill up Reese's bathtub. The water in her bath has been getting hotter for months. She just didn't notice this until she turned the hot tap all the way on and put her hand right in the stream of water. It wasn't hot to her, she couldn't get it to be hot enough. She thinks maybe she has been working up to this point for years, just losing it. She remembers being shocked at how much heat old people can stand. She just turned twenty herself, and now she is filling the tub with all hot water every day, getting deader and getting where she doesn't notice it. Maybe the water is changing, and not her. Maybe the heater is broken and no one has noticed. Last week she called Reese in to ask him if it was her or the water, and he yelled at her *Are you trying to fucking kill yourself* and she thought he was worried and the water heater was not broken. This point, after that the heat cannot increase, is pretty terrible. She switches to a harsher soap that smells nasty and lathers with suds that cling onto her, and leave her feeling scraped. This she likes, but also, she can't sleep. It might be related.

She writes a stamp letter to explain.

Dear mother, I am back in school, so you don't need to worry. However, this year I will not be joining a sorority, so I hope it's all right with you. I am okay, though. Well, here's a list. 1. Where the tiles jut out for the toilet paper dispenser in the bathroom at Reese's 2. On the sink in the bathroom at Reese's 3. On the doorknob on the front door at Reese's So I moved back into the dorms, I guess it has been one year since I lived in this town, and it is pretty much the same. Love, Julie.

The stamp letter goes on the phone bill and she mails it. She goes to class and there is a boy there she hates. She won't listen when he talks in class which is all the time, because he is an ass kisser. He never makes any sense, and as much as she hates him she keeps looking at him, because there's a jerkiness about how he walks, like everything's urgent, *how stupid,* she thinks, *relax and you'll live longer. Settle down.* But she thinks she might like to be having sex with him. The teacher makes them turn the desks into a circle maybe he thinks that'll force some of them to talk more, Julie turns her desk around and slouches back down, and never even blinks when that boy Tom is straight across from her. They're talking, the class, and this Tom has his hands gripping the front of his desk, leaning over it, like he's going to explode.

Then he fakes at her, like dogs do when they're playing, waiting with their heads crouched low over their paws, watching, and then make a move like they're going to run away or get the other dog. He does that, that same jerky thing. She sits up because he had been doing it right at her. He does it again, like he is about to jump up and run out of the class and his eyes are making looks at her, his mouth was moving a little as if he was talking, not really. So she fakes back. He's weird. That makes him smile and do it again, squeaking his desk around on the floor. No one else can notice this going on while they both start thinking it's funny. Out of the room with him — he grabs her when they both jump out of their desks around the wrist and drags her out, down the stairwell, not quite like they're racing. They can both run fast enough to keep up, neither one is faster. Tom. She looks over at him and he won't look at her maybe because she's thinking what am I doing or maybe because he forgot about her.

There they have fallen there down on the snow in their thin clothes. They get too wet and have to get up. It could be awkward the way they have to get up and sort things out after they ran halfway across campus without thinking and then just threw themselves there and so they start laughing to get to the part where they're walking. It works. They go back to her dorm and lie down on the bed. He's already breathing heavy and slower. She has her hand around his penis and it's against her cheek and her other hand on his thigh is squeezing maybe to wake him up a little, but now she's sure he's asleep. She lets the dick creep up into her eye socket, resting its head against her closed eyelid, and she can't believe she is going to sleep. It's the first time she's slept in ever, seems like. Then she can't sleep.

Julie picks up the phone. With her long legs stretched up on the desk she's comfortable, and she's playing with a hand puzzle while she's leaning back in her chair. The person wants to talk to Susan. Julie isn't good at doing Susan, makes her too wimpy, *she should be perkier* Reese says. *I'm not an actress* says Julie, *this is pornography*. Susan now is talking to the woman on the phone, she used to be a cheerleader and now she wears her uniform and drinks Diet Pepsi and eats Twinkies and never gets sick and, well, she has experienced a certain moral decay.

Susan says, *I just got back from watching the football team practice, you know my boyfriend he is number 25, but I'll never give it away to him. Our secret.*

The phone pushes up into Julie's jaw. Maybe it will leave a permanent mark . She switches ears whenever she remembers to, but she always has her face leaning down against the phone, on the cushioned plastic that is built into the receiver. She wants her hands free to work the puzzle. Reese gives them puzzles to do so they won't get bored, but Julie's just happy to be awake at night, doesn't want to go to sleep.

Let's go to the locker room, says Susan, there's music playing in there, and everybody's done changing. I'm taking off his letter jacket, I'm taking off my sweater, can you get my skirt in back? Oh. That feels good. Yeah. [Susan giggles] *Ouch, oh, I sat down on the bench — too hard. Hey, let me put your bra on instead, it's smooth, is it blue or purple? You're so thin and beautiful. I won't fit in there. The locker, ouch, ouch, oh. It's too small, lets go back to the varsity locker room, and I know I'll fit.*

Julie notices that Susan is on another line, too, over where Beryl is sitting at her desk, who is better at doing Susan, more comfortable, where she's talking about the school swimming pool and something about not getting dunked for so long next time. Susan is leading a hard life.

Wow, it smells funny back here, like men have been coming in here, I hate that. When my boyfriend comes in my mouth I spit it out in a little cup and I save it. Someday I'm going to put it into some chicken soup.... Ouch my neck, stop forcing me down into there, can't my leg stick out? There. That's nice on me, oh.

The woman on the phone puts her hand over Susan's mouth for a while, which is nice for Julie. Apparently Susan is giving head over at Beryl's desk, and since she is getting it at Julie's, it makes kind of a twisted sixty-nine. This almost never happens. Beryl is about forty, and has very short hair, maybe actually is a dyke, she winks at Julie and wags her tongue at her. They are both Susans on the phone.

The woman on Julie's line drags Susan by the arm down to the shower, hurting her very much. Then she turns on the hot water and shoves Susan under the tap, but the hot water doesn't hurt her own hand, just Susan's body.

Oh, I'm turning red, I can't take it, please please fuck me, I can't bear it, hold me, fuck me, my skin is too hot, it's hurting, my eyes I'm crying, please, says Susan.

The woman on the phone pulls Susan out of the shower and starts fucking her with two fingers on the tile floor, and it hurts Susan a lot, but not maybe as much as the shower, which could have killed her. The woman has her hand on Susan's neck as she's ramming her fingers in and out not too nicely. Susan cries a little, but actually enjoys it a lot.

Julie looks up at the clock and it's eleven. She puts the puzzle down and starts brushing her hair. Lately she's gotten interested in how healthy her hair is, not if it looks good at a certain time, but just is it healthy in general. She can't decide whether it is a good idea to brush it a lot or if it just breaks it. It distributes the oils.

The door of the office opens out smoothly and Reese is there, the boss. He's cold from outside, his black short hair is stuck straight up from taking off a hat. Reese's body is solid and big, his eyes are straight ahead, even if he's killing someone, or talking about it. He has a mad looking mouth, turned down at the corners with hardly any lips, a tough line.

Get off the phone, says Reese to her in her other ear. He's taking off his coat and is on his way into his own little office, which is off the main one, separated from the desks and girls by a glass door. Susan says *thank you* to the woman on the phone and is left tired and sore on the floor of the shower, the woman says she could pay the dry cleaning bill on her sweater, but Susan says *that's okay.*

You paid the electric bill, says Reese in the office. *Don't do that.*

You can pay me back, says Julie.

No, I don't want to pay you back. I want you to quit paying the bills that come in the mail.

Reese is reading while he is talking, won't look at her. Reese has a well made suit on, he looks great, and he still has his scarf around his neck from outside. She stands in front of his desk, her face is delicate, her smile, her body collapsible and weak, she has the thinnest arms, and the thickest hair, healthy and straight, when she really smiles it shows all her teeth.

I don't understand this, she says.

Look, he explains in a very tight control voice, kind of simpering to make her feel crappy and she likes it, *If you want to pay for your clothes with your mother's life insurance money, then fine. But I'm not going to let you pay my electric bill with it.*

I'm working. I'm making money.

You're working for me, he looks back down at his papers, not looking at her hands twisting around each other, not seeing her hands behind the desk, *that makes it stupid for you to pay the bills. Just don't do it.*

In the restaurant across from campus it starts becoming apparent Tom's not going to leave her alone about Reese. She's been telling him and telling him since four o'clock when they left her dorm room. He still doesn't trust her, he knows her really well now. He'll never trust her? Is that it?

He's my doctor, he's my doctor, she says.

Fine, he says and drinks out of his glass.

You don't understand. I only lived with him.

He eats his soup and he's taken her out to dinner. He smiles at her. He offers her a bite of his soup.

Don't give me that, she says, *I don't get it.*

Do you like yours he asks.

She throws her spoon down beside her plate and looks at the soup where some leeks are floating and the milky color in the black bowl makes her feel like vomiting. How can she eat leek soup. How can he expect her to. Tom doesn't look at her and doesn't notice her throwing down the spoon. He might think she dropped it. She takes the napkin out of her lap and throws it on the table.

What's wrong he asks.

He holds her while they are asleep. He makes her pick up the clothes in her room so it will look nice because he says she should try to be happier even if she's decided it would be a lie she should just fake it. He says this while smiling. He races her around the dorm having stolen her pen or something because he says moving around is good for the brain but she wouldn't want to get too muscular. She gets mad and sometimes laughs. He buys her perfumed hair shampoo that isn't quite as expensive as what she's used to or has, but she uses it because he can smell if she doesn't.

I'm not telling you anything about that part of my life. You wouldn't want to know anyway. I'm not telling.

Fine, he says, *Is that all you're worried about?*

Her breath is quicker and she knows it's coming. It doesn't matter if she gets mad now. Fuck.

Tom she says, *why don't you go fuck yourself you asshole. You want me to be your girlfriend and you don't even know how to have a fucking girlfriend. You don't even want one.*

Tom licks his lips and opens his eyes a few times as if someone told him something surprising. He wipes his mouth with his napkin and tells her maybe she should not talk so loud, they are in a public place. Julie's hands are starting to shake a little and she sees he's not even halfway done with his dumb soup. Fine. He wants to stay here by himself, fine. She'll leave.

Julie makes herself sit there for a few more minutes. She'll sit there, she'll keep tapping her feet together making audible noises, send it down into there, that's where she'll send it. Her hands are shaking and she gets jittery in her stomach and her back wants to twist around and she wants to twist it and crack it and bang on the table. She puts one hand in the other hand and twists one finger until she could be breaking it. She can't feel it, fuck, she can't twist enough to tell. Under the table. She grabs a piece of her thigh and pinches harder then she feels it, very hard, it's like pulling or a pressure. Tom smiles at her and is warm and kind and handsome and nice.

I'm going to the bathroom she says.

She takes the rolls off the dispenser so it won't make rattling noises and the rolls won't unravel and get on the floor and leave a mess. Her breathing takes more to blow it out than pull it in, it's very regular, very quick, and she can see there's little drops around the back of the seat. She checks the door latch. With her hands and knees, face shaking, she paces one step in the tiny stall, she can't fall over herself just pull her fingers smashing her arm down on the dispenser which is empty, until it cuts her on the sharp part.

There. Shit. Shit. Shit. Shit.

179

Her arms are flying out from her hitting on the wrists and the hollow sounding walls bang and are too dull and creak, don't hurt her, where are those arms. Shaking her head back and forth and letting her eyes go. She can feel not arms and hands getting pounded but the inside of her cheeks slapping against the sides of her teeth. There's not too much blood coming out until she can stop,   and sit down, feel something coming up warm against her skin from the inside, feeling really sleepy and aching and wanting to go home. She wipes her mouth and leans on the wall. Her hand just makes it up to the latch to pull it, lets the door fall open, in, so it smacks on her face and she feels it. She laughs. There's a woman out there with a purse by the sinks waiting and watching is she waiting to see if Julie's okay but she walks out when she sees her. *Is there a mark on my face* she thinks. I hurt myself, ouch, she wants to say, and drugged, she wants to cry or just take a bath and wash her cut up arms, not be here, maybe Tom will just take her home and she'll let him. Maybe she'll just take a little from her arms and put it into a big glass of water and mix it up, every day, to multiply it, those are different calories, exponential ones, she could drink it at night before bed and let it work while she sleeps, this drink. She decides to do it and not tell anyone.

Reese stands up from the bed and slouches, over to the dresser to find a cigarette in the dark. She's trying to be asleep now, trying to have immediately fallen asleep. The lighter flashes and clicks and he sucks, sucks. Her eyes open up and see his hand holding the red glowing stick and his body is thick and blocking the window. He has it all dark and the big window isn't even that bright, it faces away from the city. Julie's thighs hurt. Julie's head. Friendly friendly sex to come in her and make her feel it, Reese says it takes him a long time to finish and says that's good, she doesn't know, she's never fucked anyone else except for Tom at school. Takes shorter, is good sex. Julie stretches on the bed and a little moaning, to know if she's hurt, she's feeling it now, finally. Up hand, stop. Slowly up hand, fast down stop. She can't tell is he landing on the blanket, is her shoulder right there or over here or not there, is he connecting in her. Reese brings his body back into bed and props himself up so he's sitting almost, she puts a hand half clinging to his chest, half falling. She could sleep. She could let it sleep here, head on the inside of his arm, cheek on his nipple. That's over so. She could sleep here. She has sent stamp letters from this bed.

Look he says, she follows his cigarette from his mouth to the long end of his arm but that's not what he meant. *You've got to be at work on time. I don't care what happens at school. If you don't want the lines then we've got other girls, and real dykes,* he drags on the cigarette and it brightens his face and makes shadows, *wear a long sleeved shirt tomorrow — I'm tired of looking at that shit.*

Up There

His nose and his dick are both hard, and Paul is on the roof on top of the skylight looking down. With his face pressing down and his dick straight, the nose and dick are pressing up on his head and hips, but not uncomfortably. His arms and legs are stretched out as far as they'll go, and now his stomach is flat because the window is arched up toward him and shapes the stomach. In this light you can tell he's not tan except for around his wrists and his face. He's about forty-five. When his eyelashes brush on the window it makes him shiver and he doesn't like it, you see that, but he has to keep his eyes open and looking, so he can see down below where there are things going on he has to watch. You see him try to shift around and is it that his skin is stuck with some kind of glue or is gravity so much that he can't lift his head away? His hair seems limp with the snow falling in it, and too long for how curly it is. When he tries to lift his head up to blink the hair pulls down around the glass and sticks to it. His fingers uncurl, curl, his toes clench in a rhythm or he just kind of presses down on his hips or what's there.

In a room below are four men who can't get it up at all. The shrink's office has some electrical wires falling in the ceiling from under one plaster looking styrofoam tile in the corner. The light doesn't quite get back there. One of the men looks up at these wires, while the others sit in their chairs and wait for the shrink to come in. She wears neutral colors for the same reason that the room's panelling isn't too dark, but it still depresses some patients, or it calms them. When she comes in she acts like she doesn't know one of them is missing, but the short one with dark hair and a moustache points it out.

"Where's Paul?" he asks with a smirk.

"Sidney, Paul is not coming back," she answers, putting her notebook under her folding chair. She sits in on the circle, but five isn't enough to make it a real circle. Six would be enough.

One of the men, the one in the nicest suit, leans forward to take his back off the folding chair, and rests his elbows on his knees. He seems calm enough, but the one who looks the least nervous is also the youngest, wearing jeans and a burgundy silk shirt. His hair is very short and he has blue color contacts. The last one is still staring at the ceiling, now at the skylight. He has short boots on that could be riding boots, and grey pants that could be for work, or for warmth. Outside the snow is pretty bad.

"Probably got laid," Sidney says. Sidney also wears a suit but his body isn't made for that, so it bunches at his waist. Todd's body is made for nice suits. Todd's fingers cross and uncross and he has a pretty bone structure in his face.

"Do you think that would make you stop coming here, if you had sex one time?" asks the shrink, not of Sidney but of whoever.

"Hell yeah," says the youngest one, whose mouth

moves nastily when he talks, "It'd take me about a minute to figure that one out."

"It was probably that woman he was talking about last week. Geneva. She probably had sex with him," offers Todd, not looking up.

"If I had a woman..." begins the younger one, Joe.

"If you had my wife you'd know that a woman's not the first thing you want."

"Have you been able to get an erection this week, or have you tried?" asks the shrink, not directing it at anyone certain.

"Christ," mutters Rick at the ceiling.

"I'll tell you at home with my wife I don't get a moment to myself, even if I could get it up for a wank, you know what I mean?" Sidney raises his eyebrows several times at the group.

"Yeah, I got an erection, right in the middle of the stupid night," says Joe. His silk shirt is buttoned open enough to see a downy bit of fuzz on his dark chest. He has always talked about high school and standing in front of the class with a 'big-ass woody', as if it had been great. Todd has talked about dating women who ask too much, or else they expect too much, or they know too much. Sidney says his wife coddles him, and he always wonders to the group if he forgot how to have sex, like maybe if he could just remember the proper order of steps? Rick doesn't talk about anything and nobody can find out who made him come to this therapy. Nobody knows.

"You know," the shrink starts in, "Paul was always talking about how impotence of this sort, of the sort you have, was sure to be caused by a strictly physical problem.

Perhaps he found out that he was dealing with a psychological issue after all."

"With a woman like Geneva, it doesn't make a hell of a lot of difference, now does it?" Joe laughs, pulling his mouth down, and his big lips down.

"How would you know?" Sidney asks.

"I saw her, you know, hello, she was a babe of paradise."

"Big girl or little?"

Geneva paints houses not with big heavy strokes but little short ones up and down even if the panelling runs side to side - she'll fix it up later - Geneva wears painting overalls because she's so thin or because she can get them ruined with paint *God damn it* there goes another glob of peach paint down on the petunias and them striped red and white - it'll look awful - she always eats her lunch on the ladder because why go down but then sometimes she bumps the paint can with her butt and spills it the window opens beside her and there's a head of an old woman telling her *don't mind the flowers* but in a very sarcastic way so she says *okay* as if she didn't notice the sarcasm and tries to look down sideways to see how much paint actually got down there - and it's a lot - so she does try to appear apologetic but the old woman is raising one eyebrow and maybe she's funny - maybe she's okay - Geneva half smiles as an experiment and the old woman grabs her arm as if she were about to fall and laughs hysterically she's not an old woman with red rimmed eyes or messy lips with caked up lipstick in fact no makeup at all and pretty nice eyes *I'm almost done eating* says Geneva maybe to make the woman feel bad about razzing her because she knows old people don't like thin young girls not to eat and the woman props her elbows in the window and props up her chin and squints in the sun which has made Geneva all blonde and brown.

"Big girl," continues Joe, "but not too big on the tits or butt. She doesn't need them believe me."

"Is that the girl who picked him up from the bar last week?" asks Todd.

"Yeah, after... thing. Did you see her?"

"She's great. She's like a model, if they didn't want models to be such freaks. You remember Christie Brinkley? Now there."

They just can't go ahead and say Hold me back, or Easy Willie, so nobody says anything to agree or disagree. In the bar later maybe they will bring this point up again, and make some comments.

"Is that what she looked like?," asks Sidney, "Hey if my wife looked like that I'd have no problems. I mean none. You know what I'm saying?"

Joe doesn't have a girlfriend and neither does Todd. Rick has an ex-wife.

"If I had Geneva for a girlfriend... She probably sucked his dick, or something. If I had a face like that in my crotch—"

The shrink has told them to forget she is there, and sometimes they do.

"What's it got to do with her face," says Rick, "When it's not the face that counts."

He has a little bit of beard and a crisp white shirt tucked into those heavy pants. His hands are tough, not puffy like

Sidney's or smooth like Todd's. Joe's hands are small and have hair on them in tufts.

"Would you be happy with a perfect woman?" the shrink sits up straight in her chair with her legs crossed all the time, and never switches legs.

"Hell yes," Joe jumps in, "I'd be so happy then, perfectly happy."

"This is different from some of the things that you've said in other sessions," the shrink smiles a small smile without crinkling her eyes, "I wonder if you are feeling betrayed because Paul isn't here anymore and because he feels he no longer has a problem with sex."

"I'm just glad somebody's getting it," says Sidney.

"I don't feel betrayed," says Todd.

"Gee," says Rick, "I guess we all could be getting it, if we could fucking take it."

The shrink nods at Rick as if she wants them to get back on track like before Paul left and got better but he's done talking again.

"Listen," says Todd, "This just goes a long way to prove that if you had the right woman, there wouldn't be a problem. She probably doesn't make him undress in front of her, and she probably doesn't make him turn the lights out until he's ready and she probably says 'Paul, Paul' instead of 'God, God'."

"She probably does."

Maybe the rules in this city are that the bus driver gets to have sex with the very last person on the bus if it is a woman and the bus driver is a man so Geneva gets off the bus one stop early all the time and she would rather take the van everywhere that she drives at work but it's not her van and anyway she can't parallel park - not very well - so what would she do with it she is wearing black pants because she is ovulating and it leaves a spot on her panties every time which smells like the balls of whoever she sucked off last so that's why she keeps going back to her ex- boyfriend because she doesn't want her pussy smelling like some stranger the man at the corner store gives her extra lemon in her iced tea that she is buying and she says *thanks* and he doesn't let on like he knows she knows - who's looking over his shoulder - by the time she gets home her iced tea is only half gone and she puts it in the refrigerator for later where it can get tasting like the wax on the outside of the paper cup - does it seep through there - and she calls up the guy from the club which the napkin says Paul and then the number.

"What I want to know is," says Sidney with one finger held up in the air for silence, "Who here has ever gotten a real blow job, a good one, like Geneva gives?"

The shrink's eyes don't change but she looks at Rick.

"I think the kind Geneva gives is pretty rare. She uses all kinds of tricks," says Todd, finally leaning back against his chair.

"When Geneva gives head she uses just enough teeth that you know they're there."

"And dangles her boobs down there."

"And she doesn't let you come right away."

Joe laughs and shows he has a good smile.

"Maybe she doesn't let you come for a long time," he

says, "until you think you never will."

His tone has taken on a slow and mysterious tone but relaxed like telling stories around a fire at night, when you have everyone's attention. His skin is dark and smooth. He is the only one in the room without a few wrinkles.

"Now Todd here," he says, "Can make her let him come when he's ready. He might use his hand or he might not, but he's going to come when he's ready."

The men chuckle a little, and don't take offense. Todd doesn't appear to feel offended at all in fact he holds up his hand and motions them to wait as if he has a better one.

"When she goes down on me," he says, "I've got my hand on the back of her head. But I don't push," he glances around for effect, "I just feel her hair."

"Her blond hair."

"And the beauty of it is that I don't even think she realizes I could be pushing. I don't think it enters her mind."

The shrink shifts but doesn't uncross her legs. The men are accustomed to the way she looks at her watch sideways. It's not really meant to be that subtle. After a long pause the men realize that Joe has an erection.

She can taste what he has been drinking and it's good when he pulls her around the corner to try out her kissing at the same club they were at before, she can taste what he has been drinking and it tastes different and he's not making any noise, feeling her up, and his dick isn't hard thank god for her friend that came with her - to meet him here - and is waiting with the car around front for her to get done with him so this leaves it much less complicated if he doesn't even want her but why is he kissing her still and pushing down the back of her top which is a sleeveless black slutty thing - sweat on his fingers - there goes his hand again up in her hair well okay if it gets a little messy now but really she is strong and could stop him *nice tan* he says finally pulling away to look at her with her t-shirt line around her arm and she thinks is this humiliating or should I grab his limp dick and that would show him *I could suck this until it comes off in my mouth* she says for no reason but that he's still looking at her arms and he says *You have my number* - inching back away from her - and she pulls him back and bites his lips and now feels a little rise in his zipper.

"Joe, you seem to have become aroused," says the shrink.

Joe pinches his knees together and no one will look at him. His face is pinched up around the cheekbones like the erection hurts him, or like it's making his balls uncomfortable and twisted in his underwear. He looks like he wants to adjust his pants, but his hands are down by his knees.

"It would be good," she goes on, "If you could talk about what made you feel stimulated. Maybe you —"

"Hey," Sidney smiles broadly and tilts his head as if to show he understands, "Why not? He's a boy and he's thinking about a girl. He's a boy."

"Have you ever had an erection in public, Sidney?" asks the shrink.

"Me? no."

"I think," Todd's eyes don't swing around toward Joe, but he talks to Joe anyway, "Maybe you feel okay here, but when you get to where someone's all over you, you know you're going to have to make something happen."

"I think that's a good observation, Todd," says the shrink, "Could you go on? What do you mean by safe, safe from what?"

Joe stands up and is walking out of the room, and then they all look around.

"You think he's slapping off?" asked Sidney quickly.

"Hey, it's not like he's making a finger painting. You're not going to hang it on the fucking refrigerator."

Everyone looks at Rick and even the shrink seems surprised. Rick's legs are spread apart, obviously he's not hard, and his pants are loose in the hips. He has small hips, but he has big shoulders.

"That's sick, is all I can say," he says, "That guy is sick."

"Just because he got a hard on?" asks Todd quietly.

"That's not what happened. He didn't get hard for a woman."

"Geneva has a strange effect on men, you don't understand."

Rick raises one side of his lip, "When I had Geneva she didn't make me strange. She didn't make me act like a fool."

Sidney pushes his chin down into his neck, incredulous.

"What'd you do to her then?"

"I'll tell you," says Rick, sitting up straight. His light brown eyes are getting them one by one so they won't look away. "I met her at a hotel restaurant. She came in a dress, but tight all the way down to her feet and green. But there was a slit up the side. And I didn't even have to say anything. There were four buttons up at her neck and they just came undone, she took that off and underneath that was a — what looked like all messed up skin and bruises. Big bruises up here on her shoulders and fucked up down at her hips like somebody cut her, but she was smiling, and put her finger in her ear and started peeling an edge. She scratched up an edge and peeled it down, and it unwrapped over her nose and her face, down, left it so clean, cleaner than you could ever wash it. She had to peel in a few pieces, like four, but then it was all off and she had no hair and no bruises and no dirt."

Todd pulls his jacket around and buttons it, but can't sit down like that. He unbuttons it. Sidney has his face in a shocked expression and the shrink is placidly tracing the leg of her folding chair with one finger.

"When you had sex with Geneva," she says slowly, "were you able to sustain an erection?"

Rick sucks on the inside of his bottom lip and widens his eyes. He nods.

"Did you become aroused after the bruises came off?" asks the shrink.

"Then I —"

"Did you stop there or did you go on and have sex with her?"

"With Geneva?"

"That's right."

"I had sex with her."

"He did not," Sidney jumps in, "He got right up to her and his dick went like a wet spaghetti noodle."

"Hey," says Todd, "Easy there."

The toilet flushes in the bathroom next to them but since Joe doesn't immediately come back in, Sidney says,

"He must have used the one down the hall. Or downstairs."

"He probably left," says Todd.

"Are you tired?" asks the shrink, "We're just about out of time."

You see that Paul's skin will be dried out from this weather, and he is watching the men go out different doors as if he is sad to see it is over with. The snow blows around him and catches on him then blows away or makes drifts in the crevices, clinging piles around the hair. He shifts the weight with great effort off of his penis and onto one hipbone, but it quickly becomes to difficult to keep his other hipbone up so he drops back down. Inch by inch he creeps his right hand toward his face to scratch his eye, and then creeps it back out so it is extended again. Todd and the shrink are talking about something, but you see Paul is not interested in that conversation, his eyes are on Joe who has come back in the room to get his coat. Paul's forehead is so cold it must send aching pain into his head, that brittle solid cold pain. You see him close his eyes for a second after Joe leaves and then look back at Todd and the shrink. He squints his eyes from the wind and then starts creeping his hand back up again to push the hair out of his face so he can see.

She can see that the paint isn't mixed enough and stirs it with her wooden flat stick and it still has swirls of unmixed paint it's not a great brand either - today is not so sunny - the old woman has a friend over at her house Geneva can see who has thin hips and a boy about twelve who comes to the window *Can I help with that* he asks *No* says Geneva *if you fell off this ladder your grandma'd be mad at me* the boy looks down to the ground from inside the house - bending his neck over - and Geneva shifts on the ladder to show how creaky it is she's pretty high and the boy looking out is impressed and sits down so he can look out the window - the back of the house - the old woman's dog is tired on the back porch the dog has his legs around his food dish and is asleep in it but it's empty when Geneva looks down she likes the kind of scared feeling because she has both hands wrapped around the ladder whenever she looks down and she never extends it until the doubled up part is shorter than the single part - you can die - she never wants to shock anyone by falling who might be in the house at the time and anyway she used to stretch a tightrope across trees about ten feet up for the neighborhood kids when she was young and the only one who would stand up there.